Fall River

Alexander Motyl

Alternative Book Press
2 Timber Lane
Suite 301
Marlboro, NJ 07746
www.alternativebookpress.com

2014 Paperback Edition
Copyright 2014 © Alexander Motyl
Cover Illustration by CL Smith
Book Design by Alternative Book Press
All rights reserved
Published in the United States of America by Alternative Book Press

Originally published in electronic form in the United States by Alternative Book Press.

Publication Data
Alexander, Motyl, [2014]
Fall River/ by Alexander Motyl.—1st ed.
p. cm.
1. General (Fiction). I Title.
PS1-3576.A44M689   2014
813'.6—dc23

ISBN 978-1-940122-13-7
Printed in the United States of America
10 9 8 7 6 5 4 3 2 1

In Lieu of a Preface

The city of Fall River, Massachusetts, has always had a special place in my imagination. My mother—who pronounced it Foll Reever—was born there and my grandmother is buried there. And because almost all my parents' immediate family and more distant relatives lived under communist regimes in Ukraine, Poland, and Czechoslovakia, Fall River became, perhaps inevitably, the only immediate connection I had with my family history and my "roots." In time, regular visits to Fall River and my grandmother's grave and the little house on Division Street where my mother grew up became *de rigueur* and the city progressively assumed a well-nigh mystical stature as an "imagined homeland." *Fall River*, the novel, is rather more about that imagined place than about Fall River, the actual city on Narragansett Bay.

This novel is, thus, ninety-five parts fiction and five parts fact. Mike, Manya, and Stefa were real people—Manya was my mother, Maria, and Mykhaylo (Mike) and Stefania were her siblings—and they really were born in Fall River, lost their mother in 1922, traveled to Poland in 1923, and then returned to the United States in 1938 and 1947. Mike served in the Civilian Conservation Corp and the United States Army, he did have romances with two women named Myrtle and Edna, and he was in fact institutionalized in 1951. Manya did indeed have an admirer named Stefan and two best friends, Mańka and Fanka. Stefa's husband, Bohdan, was in fact tortured and killed by the Soviet secret police in late June 1941. Most of the other people and places the novel mentions were also real. Everything else—the motivations, the fears, the emotions, the expectations, the interpretations, the experiences: in other words, everything that makes a novel a work of fiction—is fictional. It goes without saying that, like any work of fiction, *Fall River* has no relationship whatsoever to truth or Truth or anything in between.

The structure of the novel is simple and straightforward. Chapter One is about Mike and it is written in the second person. Chapter Two is about Manya and it is written in the first person. Chapter Three is about Stefa and it is written in the third person. Readers are welcome to guess why and to speculate what it all means, although I suspect the exercise will prove fruitless.

It is, of course, to Mike, Manya, and Stefa that I dedicate this book.

Alexander Motyl
New York, June 2014

3

Contents

Chapter 1: Mike   7

Chapter 2: Manya   55

Chapter 3: Stefa   101

Chapter 1
Mike

When it comes to how it all began, perhaps one should begin in the eighteenth century with Joannes who married Phelagia Hykawa on February 9, 1785? Or, if lineages convey meaning and therefore demand attention, with Basilius who married Agatha Bobrecki and had six sons, Gregorius, Joannes, Timotheus, Gregorius, Demetrius, and Simeon, as well as three daughters, Xenia, Catharina, and Marianna, who married Gregorius Loik on November 18, 1827 and had three children, Demetrius, Andreas, and Joannes?

Well, this is a start, but how does one continue in the nineteenth century? With Gregorius who married Pelagia Kokot and had ten children: Ahaphia, Anna, Demetrius, Helena, Basilius, Michael, Theodosia, Joannes, and the twins Nicolaus and Anna? Or with Michael who married Anastasia Loik and had two? Or with Stephanus who married Ahaphia Szkarupski and had six? Or, perhaps, with Theodorus who married Tatianna Markow and had eight children: Maria, Basilius, Michael, Maria, Xenia, Sophia, and two Anastasias?

Somewhere from within this maze there emerges Joannes (1853-1910) who married Maria Kuzma (1858-1949). And with Joannes and Maria, the fog lifts a bit. They had five sons—Jan (July 8, 1881-June 6, 1949) and Michał (January 1, 1883-1947), who lived many years, and Mykola, Evstakhii, and Dmytro, who lost their lives as very young men in Bosnia in the opening days of the Great War—and two daughters, Kateryna (1886-1961) and Julia (1901-June 3, 1969). And it was Jan, or Ivan as he would also have been called, who married Anna, came to Fall River, and had three children: Mike, Manya, and Stefa. With them, the fog lifts some more: names begin to evoke faces and details emerge as signposts. The landscape, however, remains inalterably bleak, even after the scene shifts to America, the land of boundless opportunity, reckless dreams, and unrestrained optimism.

Regardless of what the church registers say, we know that Fall River is where it all began, don't we, Mike?

How do we reconstruct the past? The question presupposes the existence of something called the past, but its reality is hardly as obvious as human beings desperate for meaning would like it to be. The past is no thing to be grasped, no place to be visited, no scroll to be opened, read, analyzed, and comprehended. Where are the memories of the past? On hangers? On clotheslines? In safes? In cardboard suitcases? In photo albums? In pant pockets? In cupboards? Who knows? Not you, Mike, that's for sure.

What can we remember if we remember nothing? What can we claim to have experienced if we experienced nothing? Well, there are some artifacts: a few letters, two tie clips, nine army medals, one brown twelve-by-sixteen inch leather-bound photo album, twisted bits of dental wiring, and about twenty or thirty documents. It is as if we were blind archaeologists in the midst of harsh terrain. How large is the site? We have no idea. How deep is it? We don't know. Are the artifacts we discover or, more precisely, the bits and pieces of artifacts we discover—the shards, the buttons, the pointy objects, the rounded surfaces, the rusty nails, the bits of bone—parts of something we can reconstruct, that actually existed? Or are we merely imagining we have approximate notions of what we are doing and supposedly reconstructing?

These bits and pieces of a whole life resemble cat hairs on a black woolen coat or dirty wads of chewing gum on the soles of shoes. Except that even these analogies are inaccurate, Mike. In actuality, we passed each other soundlessly in the night, not even as ships that leave wakes and produce waves and cause the fish to scatter, but as two leaves that fluttered downward at different times and in different places and were then carried off in different directions by gusts of wind. And what, exactly, do these gusts of wind represent? Fate? Destiny? Inevitability? History? God? Do you know, Mike? Of course you don't. And, as all my failed metaphors attest, neither do I.

Here is one fact I do know. It is in a letter from Myrtle, who says she can still remember your singing "Smoke Gets in Your Eyes." The letter is posted in late 1945 in Augusta, Georgia, and it is written on blue writing paper in a scrawl that conveys a touching childishness and a very nuanced, a very adult despair. If letters could scream, this one would.

Who is this Myrtle? All we know is that she has a husband named Alonzo and lives in Augusta, where your army unit was based. She is—or was—your lover. You had a highly illicit affair and Myrtle is terrified of something. She sounds desperate in her letter: she says she's getting what she deserves. She misses you and wants you, but she also says you should forget her, completely and forever. And then, in her postscript, she says she remembers your singing "Smoke Gets in Your Eyes."

This is a good-bye letter that is no good-bye letter, Mike, and you know it. Myrtle wants desperately that you write back, maybe even hop the first train going east from California. She wants the doorbell to ring while Alonzo is at the factory. She wants her sweet Mikey boy to appear at the dented screen door, a crooked smile on his face, one eyebrow straight, the other at an angle, and a melody in his heart. She wants her kind and gentle Mike to plant a smacker on her hungry lips and place both hands on her round hips and rub his nose against hers.

"Smoke Gets in Your Eyes": How appropriate for you to have sung this song! Myrtle must have cried her eyes out every night. She missed your good hands and supple body. She missed your wry smile. And she knew she would never see you, your hands, your torso, your smile, ever again. She knew you wouldn't answer that letter. How could she not cry? How could the smoke not get in her eyes?

I have never shaken your hand. I have never felt your kiss on my forehead. I have never even seen you: standing before me, laughing at the far end of a table covered with holiday fare, drinking beer in a garden, dealing cards and downing shots of vodka, firing a rifle, focusing a camera. You do not exist—except on pieces of paper and in a few insignificant things. My tears, when they sometimes come, are senseless, pointless, meaningless, and absurd. If I cry, it is not because I miss you, but because I have never had the opportunity to miss you.

But I do have photographs and I do have documents. They are a start and that is something, even if that is all they are. So let us go back to Myrtle, who is far wiser and more perspicacious than she could ever have suspected.

Dec. 5, 1945
Dearest Mike,

How are things with you now? Fine I hope. Have you made arrangements for your sisters to come over yet? I hope you will all soon be together. I know it will be a happy day for you.

Mike, I'm sorry I told you my troubles. You have enough on your mind as it is. But I couldn't tell anyone else. I'm afraid to even mention you to Alonzo. I don't want him to get suspicious. And I had to tell someone, so I told you. But I don't expect you to do anything about it. Just forget I ever told you anything.

Alonzo has been very sick and is in the veterans hospital at Columbia, S.C. now. He has asthma. But I'm sure we will get everything straightened out. So don't worry about it.

And if you answer my letters send them through Eunice. But be careful what you write. And if you think best—don't write at all. Because you have a life of your own to live and I'm sure my letters will upset you.

And if you come to Augusta get in touch with Eunice and let her arrange for me to see you. The way things are, now—I'm afraid for you to come to the house.

And there's nothing you can do, if you do come to Augusta, you will only get more worried. And I'd cry and make a fool of myself. And I'd rather not.

I think it would be easier to just say good bye… and you can try to forget anything ever happened. Go on and find you a <u>nice</u> girl and settle down. But don't have 12 kids (just have 11).

Mike, I don't know what I mean. But I want you to know that I still think you're a wonderful person. And I don't blame you for anything. I'm only getting what I deserve.

But I want you to be happy always.

So forget Augusta. And the best of luck to you.

Myrtle

PS. I keep remembering you singing "Smoke gets in your eyes."

So what do you have to say for yourself, Mike? You got the dame pregnant and you dumped her, didn't you? But she still loves you and she still remembers how you'd sing "Smoke Gets in Your Eyes." What a rake you are, Mike, a rake and a bounder. I would never have guessed from the photographs of you as a teenager. Your cheeks are round and full, your hair is parted neatly and combed to the sides, your eyes resemble a rabbit's and you are wearing knickers. The overall impression is of a boy, an inexperienced and awkward boy on his first date. And then, just a few years later, there you go seducing a married woman named Myrtle in the American South!

How did you meet her? Like you, Alonzo is a soldier. Did he invite his buddy home for dinner? Did Myrtle bake meatloaf and serve it with mashed potatoes, thin gravy, and canned peas? Did she brush her hand against your warm cheek when Alonzo when to the icebox for a beer? No, that doesn't seem right. I can't see you

11

befriending an asthmatic named Alonzo and I can't see Myrtle acting so brazenly. How's this version? You met her in a bar when Alonzo wasn't around and it was love at first sight. Sure, that's it. Myrtle must have gone to the bar alone or with her girlfriends. Myrtle was on the make.

She went to a bar where the soldiers hung out and she went there to meet some good-looking grunt hungry for a hungry dame. And there you were, standing at the bar with your buddies, a beer glass in your hand, and that trademark smile, shy and bent, adorning your broad-faced Slavic mug. How could Myrtle resist? She sized you up, compared you to Alonzo, and decided that, despite his broad shoulders and large biceps, she wanted a sensitive man, a kind man, a shy man, the kind who, had she engaged in a leap of imagination at just the moment her eyes first met yours, would sing "Smoke Gets in Your Eyes."

And perhaps that's exactly what you were doing! Your buddies are horsing around at the pool table, while you're leaning on the jukebox, snapping the fingers of your right hand, and, in your awkwardly accented English, struggling to sound as hip as the lyrics:

> *They said someday you'll find*
> *All who love are blind*
> *Oh, when your heart's on fire*
> *You must realize*
> *Smoke gets in your eyes*

How could Myrtle resist? It was almost a set-up. Too bad she didn't realize she'd eventually end up humming the final stanza:

> *Now laughing friends deride*
> *Tears I cannot hide*
> *Oh, so I smile and say*
> *When a lovely flame dies*
> *Smoke gets in your eyes*
> *Smoke gets in your eyes*

12

And how could your eyes have not been full of smoke? It is 1938, you are barely nineteen and you are about to board a train for Hamburg. There, while desperately clinging to the slick railing, you will mount a ramp and become one of hundreds of bundled passengers on the President Roosevelt, a mighty American ship that will, after two weeks on the rough waters of the North Atlantic, dump you in a country that is no longer your country and a home that is no longer your home. There is a photograph of you in front of the Mickiewicz monument in Lviv: you are wearing a thick jacket and floppy cap, your pants are uncreased, your shoes look too big, and your doubtless sweaty hands are thrust deep in your pockets. It is a moment of truth for you and you look like you know it. In a few days or in a few hours you will kiss your father and your siblings good-bye, perhaps for the last time, perhaps in the knowledge that you will never touch their flesh and feel their skin on your lips again. Who wouldn't feel uncertain, who wouldn't be terrified at the prospect of negotiating an enormous body of water on one's own? And especially someone like you, who may never have been in Lviv or Lemberg or Lwów on his own?

The swastikas appear as soon as the train crosses into the German Reich. The stern customs officials and blond-haired guards greet the passengers with "Heil Hitler," they eye you suspiciously, they examine your U.S. passport and look closely at the quiet young man who claims to be heading for New York, who says he was born an American. Why doesn't he speak English? Why doesn't he know anything about the country whose citizen he claims to be? Is he Jewish? No, the face is too round, the nose is too flat. He has little money and his naiveté appears to be sincere. He is no cunning Jew. They stamp your passport and return it to you. Do they bark "Heil Hitler!" or do they wish you "*eine gute Reise*"? Do you smile or do you avert your eyes?

And then there is Edna. It is 1945 and you are already in California, in the army base at Camp Haan, just east of Los Angeles. Myrtle is still writing to you, but you are not writing back. The war is over or

13

about to end, you are still teaching soldiers to shoot rifles at distant targets, and Edna, forty-nine-year old Edna, shows up and falls madly in love with the broad-faced boy with a silly grin who is half her age. Edna has had three husbands, she has some money, she has a ranch house in a good Burbank neighborhood—quite a turnaround for a country girl from some hole in the wall in the dust fields of Oklahoma. When she dies in early 1946, her remains reach the pinnacle of earthly success and she is buried in a cemetery in Hollywood, not far from Rudolph Valentino. You could have had her, Mike, but you lost Edna to the Latin Lover.

How did you meet Edna? She has two brothers and one of them could have been your army buddy. He invites you home and there's his big sister preparing the meatloaf, mashed potatoes, and canned peas. No, that doesn't seem right. Why would forty-nine-year old Edna be entertaining her kid brother's pal? Besides, the plot is too prosaic: you deserve better than a warmed-over version of a story that didn't work for Myrtle. Would Edna, proper, prosperous, and well-fed Edna, trawl bars frequented by rowdy soldiers? If she's looking for husband Number Four, wouldn't she have gone to a country club or church dance? Except that Edna's going on fifty and is no longer the pretty young thing she used to be. Who but a GI desperate for female companionship would give her the time of day? Edna knows that her best days are over, that there's too much competition out there from the busty young blondes who shuffle their feet to Glen Miller and Sammy Goodman, and that she'll never find a suitably respectable mate again. Not in some country club, that's for sure.

Edna must have been as desperate as a lonely GI. She goes to a bar and there you are. Singing "Smoke Gets in Your Eyes"? It worked once—perhaps it even worked more than once—so why shouldn't it work again? Your buddies laugh. There he goes, that Mikey-boy, snapping his fingers and shaking his head dreamily, like a really cool cat, and mumbling the words that always get the girl. Mikey-boy, hey, Mikey! Here comes a real dish, Mikey! Heck, she could be your mother! But she looks hungry, Mikey, she looks hungry and she looks like she gives. Yep, Mikey-boy, that dame looks like she gives. That dame's a tomato, Mikey-boy. Why dontcha have a bite, huh? Why dontcha have a big bite?

What is it about "Smoke Gets in Your Eyes" that so appealed to you, Mike? The sentimentality of the music? The sadness of the lyrics? There is something about the tune that brings to mind Ukrainian folk songs: the dashed expectations, the hopeless hope, the lost love, the irrepressible tears. And understandably so: you left everything and everybody dear to you at the age of nineteen, you crossed the big blue sea with your father's suitcase in your hand and a few dollars in your pocket. God only knows how you must have felt walking aimlessly along the slippery deck, bundled in your lumpy jacket, gazing at the endless vistas of angry waves that seemed to merge with the equally menacing sky at some indeterminable horizon. There is no vanishing point. There are no gulls, no fish, nothing. There is only water and sky and clouds and spray and rain and, when a storm captures the President Roosevelt in its tight grip, the ship feels as tiny, helpless, and abandoned as a rowboat and you wonder how it's possible for several hundred cold and smelly bodies to survive the predations of a natural world intent on asserting its primacy by destroying everything that dares to take short, quick, terrified breaths.

The waves are as high as the hills of Przemyślany and the ship rises and falls and rises and falls with monotonous regularity. You're too terrified to be seasick. You hold the icy railing tightly. Your hands are frigid and your knuckles are white and you know that the smart thing to do would be to dash for the door, run to your room, and hide in your bunk, but, instead, you stand rooted to that bit of slick deck, the wind whipping your round baby-face, the salt-water spray stinging your rabbit eyes. You know you'll stand there for as long as you can, because only this monstrous display of nature's power—the pounding, pounding, pounding, the incessant pounding of the relentless waves—can soothe your soul and calm your beating heart and enable you to anticipate the future, which is barreling toward you like a wild bull, with a modicum of equanimity. Perhaps for the first time in your short life you understand just how fragile the world is and just why the folk songs they sing back home are as mournful as dirges. And then, when you first heard "Smoke Gets in Your Eyes," how could it not shake you to your core and become your favorite song?

After two weeks of somber water, impenetrable clouds, and soul-shattering storms, you enter the calm of New York harbor. Would you have remembered the last time you were there, in May of 1923, when you left America? A four-year old has only blurry memories or empty memories, almost as blurry and empty as mine, which, as you know, are non-existent. Perhaps some image, momentarily suspended in the sky like a brown leaf caught in a gentle updraft, still remained in your mind: the blaring foghorn that frightened you and your sisters, the rows and rows of quivering horses and coal-black carriages assembled on the shore like soldiers waiting to repel an imminent assault, the pain you felt in the hand your father held too tightly, the terrifying mixture of voices, screeches, shouts, bells, thumps, and tears, the fat seagulls nervously standing guard on rotting green pylons?

There is the clickety-clack of the cobblestones as the wagon arrives at the pier. There are the huge, hairy forearms of the thick-set workers heaving the suitcases onto dollies, the cavernous hall where stubby cigarettes are lit, passports are waved, and tickets are stamped, and the rubbery feeling in your spindly legs as you ascend the swaying, moaning, groaning, creaking gangway. And there is the worried look on Manya's determined dark face, the red cheeks of Stefa's, and the sweaty brow and wet mustache on your father's. You have no word for the chaos that surrounds you, but your gimpy legs on the tilting deck remind you of how it felt when you were running down South Park and stumbled, flying headlong into the thick grass and seeing the buildings, trees, and sky as if they were a merry-go-round.

16

New York, Mike, New York: you finally made it to New York! The tired, dirty, malodorous passengers and tiny, hesitant you among them push their way toward the undulating bow, hoping to be the first to catch a glimpse of the Statue of Liberty. The water is choppy, the waves no longer resemble black cliffs and gaping caves, to the right are piers the size of ocean liners, to the left, in the distance, are dull, flat buildings, but what strikes you immediately, what takes your breath away, is the multitude of boats, ships, and barges crisscrossing the harbor crazily, maniacally, almost as if they were flies or bees. Ashen smoke and white steam curl upward from smokestacks, blending with the fog and clouds that hide Manhattan like layers of gauze, until, suddenly, as the statue becomes visible on your left, monumental gray surfaces loom before you and you gasp, you crane your neck forward, and you close your eyes momentarily, because you know that, yes, you're here, you've arrived, you're actually in New York City.

The mountainous buildings sail by on your right and you espy longshoremen and sailors scurrying like ants along the piers that line the edge of the island. They remind you of ramparts, of fortifications intended to keep hostile strangers out, except that their purpose is exactly the opposite: they are there to bring you in. They are like the stubby fingers of an outstretched peasant hand, beckoning you to come inside, please, to come inside and have a seat and a glass of moonshine and a piece of dark bread. Dare you take the hand? Dare you step on shore, amid the creaking, shouting, bleating? There is no doubt about it now: you have left your home for good, you have left the stillness of Przemyślany for this madhouse, for this awful agglomeration of exaggerated sounds and sights and smells. This is another world, a wholly alien and bizarre world, and you, poor thing, are about to enter it.

The ship has cut its motor; it is being guided by small, awkwardly shaped boats with pug-nosed bows, highly placed cabins, stubby smokestacks, and low sterns. And they are painted red, as if they were intent on asserting themselves despite their preposterous appearance. This is no normal country. It is not just that everything

17

is too big, too loud, and too fast. You knew that and you expected that. No, it's that everything is upside down. The awkwardly shaped boats push and pull the President Roosevelt toward one of the stubby fingers, taking what feels like an eternity to turn the heavy, tired, sleepy giant toward the bustling shore. The side of the ship rubs loudly against the pier, like two swine in heat. There is a protracted groaning, as if some mythical creature were being awakened. Ropes are cast, foghorns and whistles are blown, passengers cheer, a multiplicity of strange tongues chatter unrestrainedly, as if they had been freed from vows of monastic silence, and down below people stand huddled between the precarious edge of the pier and the huge pale green structure that lies atop it. Handkerchiefs and hats are waved, hands flutter like butterflies. Suddenly, there is another awareness—of the stench: the salty smell of the ocean is gone and in its place there rises a fetid cloud of sweet corruption and sticky decay that assaults your innocent and inexperienced nose.

Thank God, Mike, that, as soon as you step off the ship, you will not be alone. What would you do if you were? What would you do if you had arrived in July of 1913, like your father-to-be, thirty-two-year old Jan-Ivan? The thought terrifies you at first, but then you remember he had it easy: he was immediately quarantined on some island, where they kept him for over a week, gave him American food and a bed, peered into his throat and eyes and ears and other orifices, gave him an identity, gave him time to understand just where he was and what folly he had engaged in by coming to this impossible country with only twenty-two dollars in his canvas wallet, an address in some place called Fall River, and no language whatsoever. The island must have resembled a prison: not completely unlike living in a two-room house in Przemyślany with eight brothers and sisters, two parents, and a grandmother. The smell of sweat, bad breath, urine, feces, and chloroform would have been all-pervasive, never-ending, overpowering. But a cell can also be a perfect passage way from one world to another. Like passing from Earth to Heaven by means of purgatory: isn't that how Father Kowcz might have put it?

But there is no time to dwell on Jan. He is back home, embracing Manya and Stefa, and thinking about his prodigal son, while down below, somewhere in that swirling mass of agitated humanity, is Aunt Catherine. Ciocia has been here since 1920; she has worked her way up from waiting on tables in cheap diners to selling women's hats in some large store. One of the white handkerchiefs swirling below may be hers. How old is she? Close to fifty. (As old as Edna, Mike!) On her photograph she has high, round cheekbones, a large forehead, and tight lips with narrowly focused eyes. And she is wearing a hat, jauntily slanted and adorned with a ridiculous plume. Will you recognize her if she's hatless? Will she recognize you? A fleeting sense of panic flutters through your chest. What if she decides you missed the boat and goes home? What will you do then? The crowd surges forward and you grip tightly the stained cardboard suitcase with your left hand. You adjust your cap, check the inside pocket of your jacket for your passport, and clear your throat.

The water is a muddy, opaque green; crimson, purple, and yellow patches of oil float upon it like lily pads. At the surface swirl all manner of discarded objects: jagged pieces of wood, boards, bottles, sodden bits of newspaper that resemble dirty linen, rags, dead fish. Ropes as thick as forearms strain and groan, emitting mournful sighs and occasional shrieks of surprise. A fierce wind is blowing; it slaps your cheeks and hurts your eyes. A woman to your left stumbles and falls toward you: you raise your hand and she brushes against the suitcase, mumbling her apologies in a language you don't understand. The man behind her scowls, grabs her by the collar of her threadbare coat, shoves her forward. She stops for a second and looks lovingly into his eyes, before resuming her journey downward. A seagull, just like the ones that circled the harbor in Hamburg, glides lazily from the right and disappears into the mist. The crowd before you comes to a halt and, as you pause, turning your head from side to side and extending your neck, a man bumps up against you and mutters, "*Entschuldigung.*" Like a piece of debris in the roiling waters beneath your feet, you are pushed and pulled toward the bottom of the gangway and, a few minutes later, there you are, Mike, standing on legs of rubber, standing on *terra firma* after so many days at sea and wondering just what comes next.

There is no memory, no experience of anything quite like this: the mad congestion of bodies, faces, hats, coats, shouts, groans, whistles, handkerchiefs, suitcases, trollies, dollies, workers, passengers, fingers, arms, legs, shoes, handbags, feathers, mustaches, beards. Even Hamburg was more controlled, almost sedate in comparison: there, too, the confusion engulfed you, but the barking of stern policemen, the pointing of stewards, and the self-restraint of proper German burghers kept the pandemonium in bounds. In Hamburg, there was also a clear destination: the ship that was docked alongside the gray pier. Here, the clarity is behind you, on board, in the sleeping rooms, in the dining halls, on deck, along the railing. Ahead there is nothing but cackling gulls and shouting workers and dancing handkerchiefs.

A thick man with a brush-like mustache shouts into your ear and you jump back, startled by the unwanted intrusion on your reverie. You adjust your cap, take the suitcase with your right hand, and smile wanly, but he ignores you, pushing his way to your left and waving both arms with unconcealed excitement. The entrance to the pale green edifice is to the right and, like a river, the crowd carries you toward it. Inside, the disorder is more palpable, more immediate, and the shouting reverberates within the church-like building to produce a seething, bubbling, gurgling, frothing Bedlam of mad men, mad women, mad shoeshine boys, mad clerks, mad workers. You can't possibly know, Mike, that, one day, this will be your only reality, that you will live out most of your life in just such a place. Good God, how will you ever find Ciocia?

And there she is, Mike, standing on the pale sidewalk just outside the exit, peering at the flushed faces streaming past her, a coat with a fake, brown fur collar wrapped around her matronly frame, and a tiny dog fidgeting near her knee-high black boots, yelping like a surly deckhand, and tugging at the leash in her right hand. She is staring at you with no hint of recognition: no twitch of the eyebrows, no soft smile on her lips, no sudden glint in her eyes. The cap and thick jacket make you look like an old man, a hardened worker, or a burly peasant, someone with many years of life behind him and with very few prospects ahead. You stop just before her, a broad smile appears on your face, and you say, much too hesitantly and much too quietly, "Ciocia?" She looks at you quizzically. This time, more loudly, using the diminutive favored by your family: "Ciocia: It's me, Mykhasko." "Mykhasko?" She opens her eyes with surprise. "Yes, Mykhasko. It's me." "Come to me, my boy," she sighs and enfolds you in her wing-like arms and presses you to her heaving bosom, while the nervous dog encircles your trembling legs with the leash and continues with its insane yelping.

The warmth of Catherine's expansive body soothes you and you bury your face in the soft fur of her collar and, for a brief moment, forget that the wind is still howling, that the crowds are still rattling inside your head, that the pier is still swaying under the weight of their bodies. There is quiet here. It is as if you had stepped outside the house on Pocztowa Street and sat on the bench in the garden, its apple trees heavy with fruit, the grass as sweet as a birthday cake, the stars sprinkled across the breadth of the ebony sky, the shadows as thick as honey, the stillness complete, except for the crazy chirping of crickets, the croaking of frogs, and the barking of a dog. Inside, they are all asleep: four brothers and four sisters and your mother, father, and grandmother. Your place is on the kitchen bench, near the wood-burning stove. A girl's laugh ripples through the night, from the direction of the stream and wheat fields down below. There is romance in the air.

The head is lifted from the fur. With the authority of a mother, Catherine says, "You must be exhausted, poor boy, and hungry. Come. Let's go. We will walk."

21

Is Edna Catherine? And is Catherine the mother you never had? You are born in 1919 in Fall River, Massachusetts. Your mother, Anna, dies in 1922. You were three years old and your memories of her, your experiences of her, are non-existent. Perhaps there is a mercurial image of her face. Or the lingering taste of her donuts and cakes. Or, possibly, the sharp smell of her flesh as she held you against her bosom and kissed the top of your head. Is this what you recall, unconsciously and unknowingly, as Catherine holds you tightly on the pier?

And then you leave Fall River one year later. Anna is dead, lying peacefully in a burial ground—the graveyard doesn't even merit being called a cemetery!—to the north of the city, a few yards from the glistening railroad tracks that extend southward and run past the house you live in on Division Street. The soot that rains down on you rains down on your mother and the screeching and the belching that disturb your sleep disturb hers as well. How fitting, Mike, that mother and son should share the same intrusions. But, as you're standing on the deck of the ship that is plowing its way eastward, toward Europe, in 1923, Fall River and your mother and her death and the burial ground and the railroad tracks and Division Street disappear in the mist. They become part of a past that is yours and not yours, that is real and utterly, completely unreal. On the ship there is only the ship and the endless waters, endless skies, and endless clouds. And after the ship there is the port and the train and, finally, the new house and the new street in a place your father calls home. Until you discover that fields, forests, and a stream hold as much promise as South Park and Narragansett Bay, the first weeks in your new home are as devoid of anticipation as those mind-numbing get-togethers in Fall River, when your parents and godparents drank whiskey, ate pierogis, and talked about the coal mines of Pennsylvania, while all you wanted was to go outside and play Johnny-on-the-pony.

Where is your mother, Mike? She lies dead in the North Burial Grounds in Fall River, a few feet from a fence that separates the domain of the dead from the realm of the living who are crammed

22

into drafty apartments in four-story tenements made of wood and painted white, as if white could conceal the awful lives of the Polacks and Portuguese inside. And she doesn't have a gravestone, not even a small marker, probably because it costs too much and your father has to save every penny for the big trip ahead and the new life in the old country he calls home. And besides, the dead don't care about what lies above them, do they?

The stepmother doesn't like you. She has three children of her own, she has three children with your father, and you happen to be the only male child of Anna's three children. Manya is the oldest. Stefa is but a baby. But you are old enough to be a nuisance, a permanent reminder that the poverty and hardships of life would be easier to bear if only that young brat ate less, worked more, and, God willing, went away. The bench in the kitchen is hard, but it is yours. Nothing else is. So why not go back home to the home that has ceased being your home since you were four? But what's the alternative? And what difference does it make where you will be and which bench will be yours? They are all hard.

Edna says she loves you. Edna gives you a frilly handkerchief with her name embroidered on it. Edna gives you two gold tie pins with your initials. Edna writes you a note: "Mike and Edna—Forever." Edna even buys nine hundred dollars' worth of savings bonds in your name, which is quite a lot of change in those days. Edna is head over heels for you, Mike. She has plans and you're a big part of them. The future looks bright for forty-nine-year old Edna of Burbank, California. And then, in early 1946, you leave the Golden State for New York. You must, you say: your sisters are coming and you have to be there to greet them. But they don't arrive until one year later, in 1947. Had you wanted to, Mike, surely you could have stayed in Edna's ranch house for a few more months. Instead, as soon as you're discharged from the military in early January, you head for the nearest exit: you scram. Edna pleads with you to stay, but you say you can't. "My sisters are coming" is what you tell her, but you know, as does Edna, that they are only a convenient excuse.

23

There are photographs of you, Mike, dressed in white cotton slacks and tee-shirt, slouching before the ranch house and sitting in a wicker chair, your hands draped over the arm rests, your legs crossed. The plants in the background are leafy and look tropical. You are holding a beer can and you are smiling that crooked grin of yours. Your eyes are sparkling. You look happy, like someone who can't quite believe he's gotten this far: the sun is shining, the sky is cloudless, you are sipping beer in southern California, and the woman who loves you is photographing your sweet mug. But that was in 1945, during the summer, when Edna thought she had her man, while you already knew that, in a few months, you'd be boarding a train and high-tailing it for New York. You may have remembered your first trip out West, back in 1939, and the hopes, expectations, and fears you had. In early 1946, Edna's hopes and expectations are dashed and her fears are realized. She is distraught. Her heart is broken and, sometime between your departure in January and the letter her father writes to you in April, she dies.

It has to be suicide. What else could it be? A sudden fatal illness? The timing isn't right; the coincidence is too coincidental. But suicide makes sense. Edna's Mike leaves and Edna, by now fifty-year old Edna, knows she has nothing to live for. Her Mike has disappeared and she knows he'll never return. Life seems terribly unfair, and, what's worse, meaningless. The future is barren, hollow, and futile. What else is there to do but swallow the sleeping pills and sleep? And what an irony then follows: Edna finds repose in Hollywood Cemetery, near Rudolf Valentino, who has long since been forgotten by the delectable Pola Negri, while Anna lies next to a slum and a railroad.

Los Angeles 16 Cal.
April 18-46
Dear Michael,

Just a few lines to say how we are progressing. Had to go to Court yesterday to have administrator appointed over the estate. Don is taking it over & living there now. I was over to the place yesterday & we have all your things packed up & sent to you by express so you will soon be getting them, all but the heavy pad and sleeping bag, I will keep them until maybe sometime you will come back & if you want them you can have them. They were so bunglesome we had quite a time getting any thing to pack them in. Wanted to get a wooden box for them but couldn't. Hope everything will be satisfactory. Will go over soon & settle the funeral bill, and will have a stone placed at her grave before long. The boys send you their best wishes & think you are a real gentleman. Mike we are not mad at you, nor never have been. So take it easy.

Hope you are getting along OK with your sisters affairs. Write me occasionally & let me know how you are getting along, & if you ever come back here don't fail to come see us. My desire is that God may bless you & keep you from evil.

Yours sincerely
A.J. Yancey

So this is New York! Catherine has seized your right hand and, like Napoleon, is leading you into battle. You stumble along, barely able to keep pace with her determined stride, through the jagged canyons of a city that is unlike anything you have ever seen. What are Lviv, Lemberg, and Lwów in comparison? They had shocked you with the incessant cries of shopkeepers, the leers of street toughs, the racket of horses' hooves on turtle-shaped cobblestones, the imposing demeanor of moneyed men in serious suits and felt hats, the painted faces of delicate women in shiny shoes. But Lviv is a village compared to what you see around you now. There are huge horses with quivering nostrils, gleaming black and silver automobiles, screeching trolleys, and rickety wooden carts and, as they inch along the congested streets, men, women, and children, white-skinned and black-skinned, weave in and out among them, almost as if they were playing football. The cars honk in response, the trolleys ring out, the horses grumble and neigh, but the human ants pay no attention to their protests and continue, undeterred and indifferent, with their weaving and plying amid the horse flesh, metal, and rubber. To your right and left rise monstrous buildings, gray, brown, and tan, with long streaks of soot and grime and armies

25

of glistening windows adorning their facades. A harsh wind blows, sometimes from the back, sometimes from the front, sometimes from the sides. The people tug on their hats, while Catherine pulls your hand with such force that you want to cry, "Stop, Ciocia, please stop and take me back to the ship!" But there is no going back and you know that, too.

It is at a crossing of two mighty streets that you witness a terrible accident that, your gut tells you, can only bode ill for the future. An automobile lurches forward, its horn blaring at the passers-by who run or freeze in response. A frightened horse pulling a small cart laden with potatoes jumps toward the middle of the intersection. The automobile strikes its front legs and the horse tilts sideways and falls over in all its breathtaking majesty, sighing deeply, its mouth frothing, its squirrel eyes darting from side to side. The cart overturns, the potatoes spill out onto the asphalt like dried beans, while the driver releases the reins and, with a shout of surprise, falls forward and lands atop the broken horse. People stop and point and shake their heads, others weave their way around the mess, heads lowered, eyes averted. A mustachioed policeman, his chest bursting in a tight blue uniform with two rows of fine golden buttons, waves his hands and blows his whistle. The automobiles stop, the blaring of horns stops. You watch in horror, but Ciocia tugs on your hand and says, as you turn your head and catch a final glimpse of the snorting beast, "Let's go. Don't watch. Let's just go."

The image of the poor horse remains implanted in your mind. It lies there, writhing, kicking its hind legs, raising its head for a few seconds and then dropping it to the black asphalt with a sickening thud, its nostrils flaring, its teeth bared, a bubbly white froth collecting in its mouth, its tail whipping madly, its neighing alternating between hysterical cries and barely audible sobs, moans, and whimpers. The defeated animal lies amid metal vehicles, rubber tires, excited honking, and endlessly flowing rivers of faceless, voiceless people, rushing in all directions, casting quick glances at the desperate animal, lowering their heads against the wind, and pushing forward. There is no end to the cacophony here. At home, there is no movement, while here, in this insane city, there is nothing but movement—constant movement, constant darting, constant twitching, constant flailing of arms and legs and heads and tails and teeth.

The hand draws you away, but the temptation to look back is irresistible. But there is nothing to see anymore, nothing but automobiles, carts, trolleys, and people all jammed up against one another in a massive Gordian knot. The horse lies somewhere among them. It is invisible, except for the pathetic sounds that continue to escape its tortured mouth. Your eyes look forward and your footsteps fall in line with Ciocia's. It is best to turn away and to forget, not just the horse, not just its agony, but everything. But is forgetting possible? Of course it is, as you know all too well.

Slowly but unmistakably, the city's appearance changes as you leave the skyscrapers and approach the river bounding the eastern side of the island. The hordes of vehicles and people thin out with every block, but what impresses you most is the buildings: suddenly, they are small and many are red, like the preposterous little boats in the harbor. The narrow brick structures are three, four, and five stories tall, three to four windows across. The roofs are flat, with sculpted extensions that are too narrow to serve as protection from the elements: they must be decorations. The second thing that strikes you is the pervasive filth: the streets and sidewalks are littered with newspapers, broken glass, cigarette butts, dog droppings, and mysterious black splotches that stick to your shoes. Battered garbage cans overflowing with potato peels, green bottles, glass jars, empty cans, and greasy brown paper bags, with their flattened lids sitting precariously atop the trash, line the sidewalks like disheveled, unwashed, rotund sentries. The third thing that strikes you is the people. Gone are the suits, long coats, and elegant hats that congregated around the horse. These people, the ones you encounter amid the receptacles and along the stoops, are visibly poor in a way that the poor Ukrainians and Poles you know would

27

never be: their clothes are shabby, worn out, ragged, their cheeks are unshaven, their hair is sticky and unkempt, their shoes are unpolished, and their shoelaces are frazzled. You notice the shoes immediately, of course. Your father, the shoemaker-turned-farmer, knew his shoes and he knew how to keep them in good condition. Stretch them at night, he would say, always keep them polished. They'll last longer and look better. We're too poor to be indifferent to our footwear, Mykhasko: remember that.

As you pass a tavern, a drunken man in a rumpled brown suit and no coat and hat stumbles out, pauses briefly, sways in the wind, and drops to the sidewalk before you like a sack of cement. Ciocia stops for a second, grabs your hand, and leads you around him. He is motionless; dark blood flows from his nose; his arms are at his sides; his eyelids appear to flutter. A short woman in a frayed green coat and torn stockings steps over him and continues walking. "Who is this?" you ask. "Just a bum," says Ciocia. "Don't pay any attention to him." She corrects herself: "To them."

Finally, you reach her building on East Sixty-Third Street. Here you will live with your aunt. This is what your father and Catherine agreed to, but who exactly is this aunt? She came to the United States as a child. Her mother is a distant relative, by marriage, of your father. No one in Przemyślany has seen her in thirty or more years. No one has heard her voice in all this time. Her Ukrainian is oddly accented: she rolls her R's like an American and the sentences strike even you, with your eight grades, as awkward. But her body is warm and her grip is strong. That will suffice for the time being.

What happens next? Ciocia's apartment is smaller than you imagined: a tiny kitchen with an icebox, stove, and bathtub, a toilet in the ill-lit hallway outside, a bedroom with just enough space for a narrow bed and a dresser littered with familiar women's objects—mirrors, pins, earrings, powders, creams, brushes, combs, perfume bottles—and a narrow room, more like a passage way, actually, with a radio, lamp, small table, and couch, on which two embroidered pillows occupy the corners. The three rooms are arranged in a line:

the bedroom faces the street and has two clean windows that open by lifting and dropping the panes; the kitchen faces an overgrown backyard and has one grimy window; the middle room, where you will sleep, has no window. But your first thought is that you will have more room here than at home. Indeed, you consider yourself unimaginably lucky to be able to sleep on a real mattress and use a flush toilet. You pull the chain cord, water drops down from a leaky wooden box suspended above, and the whole contraption gurgles and gurgles, almost like the stream back home.

Ciocia works every day and comes home exhausted. As she pulls off her shoes and rubs her stockinged toes, she complains about her aching feet, but you know she's really complaining about you. But what can you do? You have no language, no skills, and no work. Most of the building's tenants appear to be jobless as well: the women gossip in the hallways, the men drink, and everyone communicates by yelling. Back home they said you'd quickly find work in the land of endless opportunities, but how are you to get a job if you can't even ask for it? Ciocia tells you to go to the Ukrainian neighborhood downtown: "Just walk down Second Avenue and you'll be there in about an hour. Our people live there. Ask around. Maybe someone will know of something. OK?" You smile back and say "OK" as well.

The trek becomes part of your daily routine. There are taverns, but they need no help. There are small restaurants and stores with shoes, clothing, and books, but they are unimpressed by your sales experience and have no openings. The church already has enough janitors and cleaners. The priest asks about life in the old country, smiles weakly, and blesses you. One day, an empathetic barman gives you a few free drinks and, like the drunk you encountered on your first day in New York, you stumble outside and fall flat on your face. Ciocia scolds you and shakes her head. She is getting impatient. "I barely make enough money to feed myself," she gripes. One day, she shows you a leaflet describing something called the Civilian Conservation Corps. "They'll teach you English and give you a skill and you'll have a roof over your head and a full belly," she says. "You'll even make a little money." It is settled and, in April 1939, after four months of soulless inactivity, you enlist.

Days of endless rattling in an endless train headed for a faraway land called Oregon. You enunciate each of the syllables—O, Reh, Gon, O, Reh, Gon—and turn them over in your mouth as if they were hard candy. Your half-closed eyes see rounded mountains, verdant hills, an infinitely expansive steppe with fields of wheat and corn, and, finally, snow-capped mountains, dark pine forests, and deep valleys, all punctuated by stops in mysterious cities and dusty towns that, for you, are only unpronounceable words. The vastness of this country upends all your expectations. The windows are streaked with dirt and they cloud your view, dulling the bright blues, yellows, and greens, but you gaze incessantly nonetheless, avoiding eye contact with the other recruits, declining swigs from the brown jugs being passed around, escaping from the incomprehensible chatter surrounding you. "Hey, Mike! Hey, Mikey! C'mon, have a swig, Mikey-o!" You smile and say, "Tank you, no, tank you." "Aw, c'mon, Mikey, c'mon, have a swig!" You shake your head and smile again, turning your head slowly toward the window and the speeding landscape that makes your head spin and intoxicates you.

    At night, on the top bunk, sleep doesn't come. The rocking of the ship was like a lullaby and you slept easily and innocently. The train jerks and shoves and pushes and pulls and your tired body feels like a fish flapping desperately on the deck of a small boat. Lights and shadows rush across the ceiling, the screeching of the wheels jars you awake just as you are losing consciousness, and the heartrending loneliness of the mournful train whistle keeps your mind awake and your thoughts focused on the land, the town, the house, the people you will never see again. Fragmentary images, no longer as vivid as they were several months ago, flit before your eyes. It is like watching a silent film with Chaplin's jerky motions amid constant fade-outs. Is that your father? You are no longer certain just how long his mustache is. Is that Manya? Is that Stefa? Or are these the faces of women you've seen in the Ukrainian church on

Seventh Street? The house looks larger, whiter; the street looks longer; the town appears quieter. Where are the shopkeepers? Where are the Jews with their side locks and yarmulkes? Where are the horses and carts? The town is empty and the house is empty. Only your father, Manya, and Stefa are visible, but just barely, almost as if they were ineffable apparitions of the night. They are waving their hands and smiling, for no apparent reason. Is that you next to them? Yes, it might be, but they no longer see you and you are neither smiling, nor waving. You appear to be a ghost, which of course you are. You do not exist, which of course you do not.

There must have been mixed feelings, Mike. On the one hand, there is freedom, independence: you are finally leaving home and becoming a man. On the other hand, there is fear and trepidation: for the second time in just half a year, you are leaving home and being forced to become a man. That may be too much for a pudgy boy from Poland. But there is no alternative, of course. There is as little for you to do in Ciocia's apartment on East Sixty-Third Street as there was on ulica Pocztowa in Przemyślany. Your presence on this train is inevitable and your arrival someplace in the mountains of O-Reh-Gon is just as inevitable. And yet, you sense there is also great possibility. The Americans speak of opportunity, but that is not quite what awaits you. The world has opened, in far too hurried and painful a way, but, suddenly and for the first time in your life, the impossibility of life has become its opposite: possibility. The landscapes, the vast and endless steppes, are a reflection of what life holds in store for you. Possibly everything, possibly nothing, but, wherever you eventually land, you know or suspect it can be anywhere. How could you know, as you lay on your bunk and listened to the rush of the train and the staccato-like rhythm of the wheels rumbling along the tracks, that, one day, you would arrive in the very opposite of the openness that surrounded you at that very moment, that you would spend half your life within the lily-white confines of mental wards?

31

Was the train ride when you first heard "Smoke Gets in Your Eyes"? Did one of the boys sing it as you sailed along the prairies? Did it resonate with the sadness in your heart and the pain in your soul? "Sing it again, Jack," someone says and, this time, you hum along. After a few more times, you know the words or, rather, you've memorized the words. Their meaning is as hazy as the mists that hover above the wheat fields in the morning. But you know you are singing about love, about lost love, about pain and tears. By the time the train reaches the Rockies and wends its way along curved valleys and steep mountains, the boys say, "Hey, you guys, how about singing 'Smoke Gets in Your Eyes'?" Your tenor goes well with Jack's baritone and the boys applaud and whistle when you are done. "Good job, Mikey," Jack says. "Where'd you learn to sing like dat?" "Een choir." "In a fuckin' church choir?" What is there to say to that but to smile?

Jack is from a mining town called Shamokin. His mother is Slovak and his father is Polish, or it may be the other way around, and he speaks a mixture of both languages that is comprehensible only to you. There was no way he was going to go down into the hole, as he calls the mine: no way, Jose. An older brother did and he can't imagine life beyond the mines and mills of eastern Pennsylvania. Jack almost finished high school and he had enough education to know he wasn't going to become a miner: no way, Jose. Besides, there was the Depression and they were closing the mines anyway. Jobs were tight and, when he learned of the Corps, how could he not sign up? "Me too," says Mike. "All of us are like dat," Jack says, "we're all looking for opportunity." "And posseebeeleetee," says Mike. "Same ting," says Jack, but, even with your limited knowledge of the language, you know they're not the same thing at all.

As the train barrels across America, you have no way of knowing you are two or three years away from meeting Myrtle, the simple girl from Augusta, Georgia, who will immortalize your love of "Smoke Gets in Your Eyes" in a postscript to a letter that you, sentimental slob that you are, will save among several other mementoes from your short life in the world of the living. Myrtle is probably already married to Alonzo, her soldier man, and she is probably already wondering what the hell could have driven her to walk into that lousy set-up with her eyes wide open and her hopes so thoroughly focused on the brawny soldier whose mouth smothered hers and whose large hands caressed her curves in a way she had never quite experienced before.

What ever happened to Myrtle after you stopped writing or she realized the futility of writing? Did she kiss and make up with Alonzo? Did she dump him while he lay in hospital recovering from his asthma, board the first bus going anywhere, and get a job as a waitress in some greasy spoon, hoping the boss wouldn't notice her belly until she saved up some dough? Or, maybe, Alonzo came home and found some trace of lover-boy Mike and beat the crap out of her and she lost the child? Or, maybe, Myrtle finally decided she'd had enough and swallowed too many sleeping pills and never woke up? You'd never have known, Mike, because Alonzo would never have written. After you heard about Edna in 1946, the thought must have crossed your mind: Good God, first Myrtle, now Edna. Does every person I love commit suicide?

Of course, not, Mike: there are Manya and Stefa and your father and your half-brothers and half-sisters. There is Jack from Shamokin. There is, for the time being, Aunt Catherine. All is well with them. All is well with you, too. Except, of course, that eventually they do all die, but that happens even in the happiest of stories, which yours, obviously, decidedly is not.

There are no memories and no experiences of Oregon, but there are photographs, many photographs, eighty or ninety or one hundred, all neatly pasted in an album that you kept from the first day of your arrival in Camp Squaw Creek near Gibbon. The photos are all evenly arranged, like soldiers, in three rows and three to four columns. Sometimes you pasted them in at angles, but always symmetrically, always exactly. Despite the album's having passed

33

through so many hands at so many times, not a single photo corner has come loose. You are not only a meticulous bookkeeper, Mike, as careful as possible to keep an ordered account of your past, of your experiences. You are also a recorder: the photographs are obviously yours, captured with a camera that you must have bought in San Francisco, the last stop of your transcontinental journey. There are shots of the fog rolling in from the Pacific and of the Golden Gate. Then, after you arrive in Oregon, there are multiple shots of landscapes—mountains, forests, lakes—of the barracks, of your buddies posing with beer cans—goofy grins on their open faces, their arms and legs extended—relaxing, working. There are even a few shots of you with a jackhammer, a cliff in the background, a cloud in the sky, and a floppy hat perched above your smiling face. You look happy and your buddies do, too: the cat driver Curly Maul, the forestry clerk Mike "Spitz" Pizzanello, the jackhammer boys Johnny, Thomas Buck Haley, Charles Hrab, Gus DiDrio, and Hank Cerra. You're just a bunch of regular guys having a good time working up a sweat in the backwoods.

Why this fascination with photography, Mike? Did you want to remember everything you experienced in this strange new land? Did you want to leave a record of your existence for posterity, perhaps in the subconscious foreboding that, one day, that existence would be cloistered from the world and transformed into a kind of active vegetation punctuated by visits from your sisters and their husbands? Life in Przemyślany could not possibly have engendered in you that delightful American fetish, optimism. So many deaths, so many illnesses, so much hardship, so many frustrations—even the experience of sleeping on a hard bench in the kitchen day in and day out—must have inclined you to dark dispositions and black moods. You never smile in your photographs as a boy; you smile and laugh only in your photographs in Oregon. The long train ride to Hamburg, the even longer ocean crossing on the President Roosevelt, and the trek to the Rockies must have erased so many torn memories that, soon after returning to New York, you were determined not to let the present dissolve irretrievably into the past.

34

And you succeeded, Mike, so much so that, when you came back to Catherine's in 1941, you let her take a few pictures of you on the roof of her building on East Sixty-Third. And there you are, a totally different Mike: no more baby fat, no more uncertainty in your eyes, no more awkwardly shaped clothes, and no more drooping arms with curled fingers uncertain of what to do with themselves. This time, you are wearing pressed slacks, a dapper blazer, and a white shirt and tie and your fedora is tilted daringly over your right eye. You are on top of the world, Mike. You have been transformed and the promise of possibility has, quite obviously, been fulfilled. You even pose with Catherine's little dog, knowing full well that its ridiculous size will only underscore the full man you have become.

It is in Oregon that you kiss your first girl. It is there, surrounded by your buddies, that you acquire a voice and learn to speak, and it is there that you discover that your smile, eyes, demeanor, and accent are irresistible to the ladies. "Smoke Gets in Your Eyes," you realize, is not just a song that reminds you of what you lost. It is also a means of getting the girls to look at the slight young man who is quiet and withdrawn, but has a beguiling voice that does the flirting for him.

But, mostly, Oregon is about work and beer and growing up at breakneck speed amid the unchanging environment of snow-covered mountain peaks, undulating carpets of fir trees, white cliffs, and cold streams. Two years later, in April 1941, you leave the Corps and return to New York with a little money in your pocket. War has broken out in Europe and Poland is no more. Przemyślany is now Soviet: the secret police has disbanded most of the community organizations you once knew and it is actively hunting down your friends in the resistance movement. A steady stream of letters from Manya, Stefa, your father, and other relatives keeps you informed of goings-on at home, but their growing reticence about life in general leads you to suspect all is not well under the Russian occupation. And how could it be? These are the same people who have been oppressing your nation for centuries. Ciocia says you should forget the old country—there is nothing you can do, anyway—and concentrate on finding a job: "You are an American now, Mykhasko. So think like an American." "I will," you reassure her, "don't worry. I have skills now. I have experience." "But quickly," she says. "I can't support you on my wage."

It is the same story as before. You are sleeping on the couch in her living room and her constant presence reminds you of the freedom you once had: every day is witness to the progressive transformation of possibility into impossibility. Just as your confinement is becoming unbearable, however, you find work as a machine-operator in a tool-and-die factory on Broome Street. There is money and Ciocia's mutterings cease. But the job is deadly. As the sunlight illuminates the swirling particles of dust, you stand at the same machine in the same room with the same gnarled men doing the same work every day of the week, every week of the month. What a contrast to the expansiveness of Oregon. It is time for a return to possibility again and, on January 6, 1942, on Ukrainian Christmas Eve, while Catherine is at Mass or buying beets for the borscht, you enlist in this man's army.

What made you do it, Mike? Pearl Harbor? The dead-end job on Broome? Ciocia's cramped apartment and smothering embraces? The desire for adventure? All of the above? The transition from the Corps to the military can't have been too difficult: the same discipline, the same uniforms, the same barracks, the same hard work. And the same photographs: there is no break in the album between your Oregon photos and your army photos: the same grins, the same buddies, the same angles, the same camera, the same careful arrangement, the same neatly glued photo corners. You appear only in a few shots, but always with the identical expression: broad smile, white teeth, furrowed brow, dark curly hair, champagne eyes. Once again, you are intent on recording as much of your present and as many of your memories and experiences as possible, almost as if you suspected these black and white pieces of stiff paper with corrugated edges would be all that remains of you.

You become a rifle instructor and a staff sergeant, but they don't send you overseas, despite your knowledge of two European languages. Lucky you, Mike: you didn't have to put your sharp-shooting skills to practice and avoided getting blown to bits in Normandy or Anzio. As the world erupts in full-scale slaughter, you embark on a four-year Odyssey in January 1942. It takes you to Fort Dix, Fort Eustis, Fort Stewart, Camp Haan, and Camp Roberts and lasts until January 1946, when you are honorably discharged and return to New York. This time, you really get to see the whole country: New Jersey, Georgia, Virginia, California, and all points in between. Once again, you go West, almost as if it were your fate to experience the wide expanses and silent mountains you never saw back home.

The regimen is always the same—barracks, tents, reveille, mess halls, mess kits, inspections, latrines, marches, drills, knapsacks, grub, lights out—but the sense of unlimited possibility is with you again. It may even be that the regimen enhances that sense of possibility: when everything around you is changeless, how much easier it must be to appreciate the possibility for change that is immanent in everything. There are days when you sleep outdoors, in a foxhole or on a field, and above you is spread the vastness of the firmament and the infinity of the stars and, although you have seen the same sky and the same stars many times at home, they have never seemed quite as inviting as now. Because now, unlike then, they flicker with possibility and beckon to you.

But the army is also about going out with the boys, getting smashed in off-base bars, and meeting dames. Your pals dance something called the jitterbug that is unlike anything you've seen before. All their body parts move in unison, both rhythmically and chaotically, as if an explosion had propelled the hands and arms and legs and feet and knees in opposite directions, while some unseen force keeps them from flying apart. The Americans move with remarkable ease: their pant legs flap against their shins and their ties swing from side to side and, despite their sweaty torsos and beating hearts, they smile serenely, knowing they are in complete control.

The girls perform their acrobatics with a shameless abandon. It is impossible not to blush at the sight of so many high kicks, bare thighs, and lace underwear. But the jitterbug is not your strong suit. Your body doesn't listen and, whenever you venture onto the dance floor, the effect is like that of an oversized child trying to do the Viennese waltz. Your voice, on the other hand, can win over hearts far more effectively than your legs. The others swing, while you lean against the jukebox, snap your fingers gently, close your eyes, and croon.

Myrtle is crouching at the curved tin bar, a highball in her hand. Her shoulder-length hair is blonde, her full lips are ruby red, and her canary-yellow dress caresses her strong thighs. She is anything but pretty: the nose is too long, the eyes are too large, the cheekbones are too pronounced, and the neck is too thick, too sinuous, like that of an athlete. Still, she projects a feline femininity, a disturbing amalgam of ferocity, ugliness, and eroticism that the grunts find irresistibly attractive. When she saunters past them, they leer and whistle and point and then she swings her full hips with still greater gusto.

As Myrtle is resting her elbows on the bar, she casts her eyes in the direction of the jukebox, where a slim soldier with wavy hair is snapping his fingers and singing quietly. The needle reaches the center of the record, pauses, rises abruptly, and swings back to its place with a click. The record is brought to a vertical position. It remains suspended for a second and then recedes into the innards of the music box. The soldier rummages in his pocket and finds some change. He drops a nickel into the slot and mechanically presses two buttons. A few seconds later a record drops onto the turntable and the same song that entranced him begins playing again:

They said someday you'll find
All who love are blind

She places the glass on the counter and sashays toward the jukebox. You see her through your half-open eyes and you think: "Works like a charm every time."

Myrtle turns out to be far less the *femme fatale* she pretends to be. She works in a five-and-dime flipping burgers, she lives in a two-room shotgun house in the poor part of town, several streets from the Negro section, and she is married to a big soldier named Alonzo she insists she no longer loves. "Only you, Mikey, only you!" It doesn't take you long to realize that the mascara, the lipstick, the rouge, and the eyeliner are just a mask behind which a sad, little, frustrated army wife is hiding. "You're fonee, Myrtle." "I know, Mike, but ya can't blame a girl for tryin', can ya?" "You're just like me." "Are you also a phony?" And she laughs as she runs her fingers through your forelock. "Alonzo's almost totally bald." "Give me a kiss, Myrtle." She laughs again. "Sure, Mikey, here's your *keess*. And then sing that song again for me, will ya?"

Your army buddies call them niggers and you do, too. They remind you of peasants back home. They move slowly, deliberately; they have big, awkward hands with thick fingers and big, lumbering feet; they look up from beneath furrowed brows; they appear to agree with everything that is said to them; their clothes are old, torn, and loose; and they are as often barefoot as dressed in distended shoes, the sight of which would make your father cringe and shake his white head in dismay. There are no niggers on the base, except as cooks, janitors, grass cutters, garbage collectors, and hedge trimmers. When they speak, they produce incomprehensible sounds consisting of vowels that are as distended as their footwear and limbs. It is best to smile in response. Myrtle dislikes niggers, saying they're just savages with no culture, upbringing, and refinement. "You treat them just like Polacks treat us." "But you're sweet, hon," she protests, "not at all like them." It is best to smile in response.

One day, Johnny, a soldier from Texas who speaks with a drawl that resembles the language of niggers, extends his foot just as a little nigger is hurrying along. The boys have been drinking and they're standing outside the bar, smoking and whistling at the girls and cracking jokes you don't understand. The little nigger stumbles and falls to the sidewalk. Your first impulse is to extend a hand, but the others break out in waves of laughter and you know you dare do nothing. And then you see the difference between them and us. The nigger gets to his feet and, amazingly, excuses himself and, smiling so weakly that even his white teeth don't show, runs off. This, you think, would never have happened at home. The Ukrainian would have waved his fist and gone for his friends. There would have been a brawl and some Polish heads would've been cracked. And, you think, we don't have it half as bad as the niggers. Why don't they fight? Why do they always smile? And then it strikes you: they're like terrified dogs that have been systematically beaten. They slink along the walls with lowered heads and tails. The Poles, Russians, and Jews want us to be that way, too, you think, but we have a backbone and a will. We will not submit.

Myrtle couldn't resist. Neither could Edna. Nor could the others, the ones between Myrtle and Edna, and there must have been others. But Edna's the one you fall for, too, at least for a while, at least until her embraces begin to smother you and the miraculous sense of possibility that has accompanied you for so many years begins to fade again. Once that happens, it is time to go: to let her go and to move on. Edna must have sensed your agitation. She must have known she was losing her man, her Mike. And she did the only thing she could do: she tried to draw you in with gifts, tie clips, money, a house, her body. But that only made things worse. You resisted, but the more you resisted, the more she tried. It was a lost cause and Edna couldn't win. After three husbands, the dame should've known better.

Did you actually tell her it's over or did your relationship decay to the point that it became obvious even to star-struck Edna that the world was about to end? Or did you just say you had to return to New York, that you'd write and come back as soon as everything was settled with Manya and Stefa, while intending all along to write that it's over or, perhaps, never to write? It doesn't matter, of course, not in the final analysis, because, whatever your rationalizations, you dumped Edna and Edna took it hard, so hard that she turned off the light, refrained from setting the alarm clock for six-thirty, lay back in her fluffy bed, and waited for the sleeping pills to take effect.

There must have been guilt, Mike, serious, throbbing, deeply rooted guilt that, like a tooth ache, would not go away regardless of how often you told yourself that you had no choice, that you had to do what you had to do, and that Edna had to do what she had to do. Your logic was impeccable, but the gnawing sense of guilt would not dissipate. And how could it? Edna died. The woman who said she couldn't live without you stopped living once you left. How were you to know she meant it literally? You couldn't. Even so, there must have been guilt and it would not dissipate.

Well, it is early 1946, Mike, and here you are, back in New York City. But, this time, you are living in a tenement on East Eighty-Ninth Street and not with Aunt Catherine. What happened to Ciocia? Did you quarrel? Did she move? She's not listed in the 1946 Census as living at the Sixty-Third Street address. There are rumors of suicide, but there are no distinct memories, no indisputable proofs. It's only hearsay, so who knows, but it's eminently plausible hearsay. After all, how could she have just disappeared? Where would she have gone after twenty-six years in New York? Back to Przemyślany? Unlikely. Married? Not at her age. A deliberate overdose prompted by creeping despair at being an old maid with a dead-end job? Why not? Suicide would mean that the two motherly women in your life both ended theirs within weeks of each other. There wouldn't have been any guilt over Catherine, but the shock must have been fantastic nonetheless. To lose three mothers in twenty-seven years would be too much for anyone and not just for a sensitive boy who grows teary while humming a song about lost love. It was small consolation for Edna's father to have called you a "real gentleman" and given you a standing invitation to visit him and

41

the boys in Los Angeles. At least you knew where Edna lay buried. But where was Catherine? In some Potter's Field? In New York's equivalent of the North Burial Grounds?

Manya arrives in early 1947. Stefa and her boy come later that year. But what did you do in 1946? The year is a blank. Their passage cost several hundred dollars and you paid the entire amount—probably with the nine hundred dollars' worth of bonds Edna left you. Were you working? You knew the language by now and were no longer a stranger to New York. Nor were you a kid wet behind the ears. Perhaps you took the same machine-operator job on Broome? It would've been back to the same old grind for you if you did. No more California, no more Myrtle, no more Edna, no more possibility. There remained only one reminder of the good ol' days: drinking with other vets in the German taverns of Yorkville or the Ukrainian bars off Second Avenue. Most of them had served overseas and, when you told them you were a rifle instructor in these here United States of America, they'd say, "Lucky stiff," and mean it.

The stomach pains begin around this time. Regardless of what you do, they, like bad memories, don't go away. They meander throughout your gut, sometimes lodging in your intestine, sometimes in your colon, and sometimes they are everywhere at once. Then the pain becomes so unbearable you could almost scream. It's worst when you're at work and have to concentrate on pressing the right button or pulling the right lever at just the right time or sliding the sheet of metal just the right way beneath the press. There can be no pausing, no grasping your gut with both hands, no screaming silently. Your buddies say that the pains are typical: all vets have them, so don't worry, they'll go away. "Have a drink, Mike, and forget it." The alcohol helps, but only for as long as you're drinking. Then the pains return. The doctors at the veterans' hospital say it's all in your head. You're healthy, as strong as an oak, but the war years, well, they had their toll. "Just be patient," they say. "Things'll be fine soon enough. Just be patient." But you know better. There were no war years. Your body is healthy. The pains are in your soul. They can't be fixed just like that. Souls require

42

redemption, after all, and not curing. You learned that many years ago from the saintly Father Kowcz.

In 1947 you are all together again, living in three minuscule rooms on East Tenth Street. Yorkville is too far away from the Ukrainian neighborhood and your sisters and the boy and you as well need to be closer to people who speak your language and share your memories and experiences. The church and the school are a few blocks away, as are the stores, choirs, clubs, bars, and credit union. It is almost like being back in Przemyślany again. There's a Polish church on Seventh Street, the Ruthenian church is down the block, and the Jewish neighborhood, with all the food shops and synagogues and cheap clothing stores, is just past Houston. Some of the shopkeepers are from your home town and speak Ukrainian. All of them speak Polish. It is 1947, you know that for a fact, but it could just as easily be 1937. Time appears to have stopped and, when you walk along the streets, you are a round-faced boy again. Did you ever leave home? Was there a war? Did you serve in the military? It's all a blur. And with Manya, Stefa, and her boy around, you become, at one and the same time, both an uncle whom the boy adores and a little brother. Manya is much older; Stefa has been married and has a child. You are a kid in comparison.

They find work, but you quit your job because the pains in your gut keep getting worse. The Veterans' Administration rejects your repeated requests for treatment and you're at wit's end. They owe me, you think: I gave them four years and now this! Manya, Stefa, and the boy are away for much of the day, while you sit at home or take extended strolls among the tenements, inhaling the smells of the First Avenue Market, sitting on hard green benches in Tompkins Square Park, or hoping that some pal might spring for a beer at one of the local watering holes. There are no more Myrtles or Ednas and there is no one to listen to "Smoke Gets in Your Eyes." There are days when you think back to the endless train ride across America in 1939, to the staccato bursts of the jackhammers at Camp Squaw Creek, to the drills, marches, and firing ranges in the

43

army. That is all gone now, over and done with, and there are only vague memories and even vaguer hints of the pregnant possibility you felt in your gut and in your fingertips on a daily basis. That is all gone now, over and done with, and all that remains are the pains in your gut and the hard green benches in the park.

But there is, still, the camera, the blessed, wonderful, magnificent, God-fearing camera you bought in a pawn shop in the Mission District. The album, with neatly ordered shots from your days in the Corps and the army, is full and, if you only had the money, you'd buy another one. Film is expensive, but there is nothing to stop you from wearing the camera strap around your neck and shooting without film. It is like freezing time, if only for the millisecond that precedes the closing of the shutter. And it helps you recapture some sense of will, of power, of potential. Film is unnecessary, after all. The celluloid is just an accessory. You know that what matters most to the true photographer is the experience of looking through the viewfinder, framing some bit of reality, and hearing the awe-inspiring, incredible click. What happens afterward and whether or not the image actually finds itself transferred to paper is irrelevant. The image and the click-click-click remain in your mind, where they are indelibly imprinted. Your bar buddies laugh, but you know better. You see things they couldn't possibly see or even imagine. It was, you realize, always this way, even at home.

And sometimes, on those rare days you have money, you even take what others consider to be real photographs. There is a shot of the sisters and the boy in the kitchen of your apartment. They sit in aprons, listless expressions on their faces, while the boy stands with questioning eyes next to the coal stove. There is also a shot of the boy, in mid-stride, in front of your building on Tenth. He is wearing your army cap and he looks quietly proud: proud of the cap and proud of the uncle who is photographing him in the cap. And there are two shots in the wintertime: one of the two sisters and the boy on the corner of Tenth and Avenue A, with the park to their right and snow on the sidewalk, and one of the three in front of the Boys Club of America building on the diagonally

44

opposite corner. They are wearing coats and hats and are wrapped in scarves and look warm. Their boots glisten like snakes.

But there are no photos of you. They are, you think, unnecessary. I am just a ghost, a shadow. I record reality and freeze time. There is no point in placing me within recorded reality and frozen time. Besides, how could a ghost remain a ghost then? And wouldn't the photos capture the pains in my gut? No, there is no need for that.

Remarkably and quite unexpectedly, when you point the camera at some object or person in your neighborhood and peer through the viewfinder, you see with ever greater frequency, not hard green park benches or crumbling tenements or shiny cars or dented trash cans overflowing with potato peels and rotten tomatoes, but the forests, mountains, and skies of Oregon, Georgia, and California. Manya and Stefa pose on the corner of Tenth and Avenue A and, incredibly, you see Myrtle and Edna instead. They smile seductively at you, they wave their hands, they blow kisses, they show off their legs. The effect is uncanny, but indisputable. The click-click-click brings your past back to life; indeed, the camera is a window on all that you have seen and experienced and all the women you have loved and who have loved you. How wonderful, you think, how magical to possess such great power. It is and will remain your secret, of course.

There are days when the viewfinder reveals nothing. You look at the Boys Club and you see the Boys Club. You point the camera out the window at the Russian-Turkish Baths and you see only the old Jews entering and leaving the gloomy building. You ask the boy to make a muscle and you see the boy making the muscle. It is on those days that the pains in your gut are worst and the camera has none of the palliative effects you know it can have. But, thank God, on most days the camera lets you see past the drab, limited, and distorted reality around you and catch a glimpse of the real world of possibility. Once you pointed the camera at a taxi and there, suddenly, was the train that rumbled across the prairies and whisked

45

you out West. Another time, you focused on some church and, much to your surprise, saw the cliff you and Johnny and Buck and Chuck and Gus and Hank had attacked with jackhammers a lifetime ago. It was hard to tear yourself away from the view, but the pedestrians jostled you, your camera almost fell to the ground, and you realized that the hammering you heard may have been coming from within your head.

Best of all, the pains in your gut cease when you look through the viewfinder and see the people and places of your past. Poor Myrtle! Lord knows what Alonzo did to her after returning home from the hospital. You abandoned her, you know that, but now, here on Tenth Street in New York City, you finally have the opportunity to make amends. And what better way to cheer up the ol' girl than by crooning "Smoke Gets in Your Eyes"? There is no jukebox and no bar this time, but any bench in Tompkins Square Park will do. You sit there with your eye glued to the camera, you snap your fingers lightly, and you sing the song that won Myrtle's heart. She smiles and you can see her smiling and brushing the golden hair from her face and turning her full thighs toward you. Does she forgive you? Yes, she forgives you. There can be no doubt about it. Myrtle forgives her Mike.

And poor, poor Edna! Had you only known she was serious when she said she couldn't live without you! But how could you have known? But this time you do. Edna's eyes are moist from tears of joy and she is waving the handkerchief with "Edna and Mike Forever" embroidered on it, but, instead of jumping on the train and blowing kisses through the window, you follow a whim and decide to stay. How can you resist turning to dear, sweet, precious Edna and telling her that you, too, can't live without her, that you've decided to stay with her until death or the Hollywood Cemetery do you part? Her face breaks out in a broad smile and she throws her arms around your neck and you know for sure that, this time, there won't be any suicides and that A.J. Yancey won't be writing letters calling you a "real gentleman," as if that could possibly make things better when the woman you loved and who loved you lies rotting in some grave in Hollywood, even if it is close to Rudolph Valentino and even if he is the Latin Lover. There can be no pain, not in your gut and not in your head, when you nestle your head in her bosom.

It is raining and cold outside; the sisters are at work and the boy is in school. You are sipping cold tea at the table in the kitchen. The stove is to your left and the ice box is to your right. A loaf of dark bread stares at you tauntingly from a plate. A newspaper with Cyrillic lettering, a small pot of sugar, a salt shaker, a stick of soft butter, bread crumbs, and a serrated bread knife complete the terrifying picture in front of you. It was just like this at Myrtle's and at Edna's and it suddenly strikes you with great force, almost like a punch to your gut, that you miss them terribly. I had it all, you think: women, friends, work, money, and possibility. The yellow light flickers for a moment and, as if on cue, you rise from the table, retrieve your camera from the dresser in the other room, and return. You raise the camera to your eye and look through the viewfinder. There, assembled at the table, are Myrtle and Edna and all your Corps and army buddies. They are drinking beer and laughing and flirting and dancing the jitterbug and motioning to you to join them. A crooked smile crosses your face as you close your eyes and place the camera on the table. You rise, extend your hands, and open your eyes, but the room is quiet and there is no one there. The smile vanishes: you close your eyes again and, as you begin snapping your fingers, you sing:

> *So I chaffed them and I gaily laughed*
> *To think they could doubt my love*
> *Yet today my love has flown away*
> *I am without my love*

Myrtle, Edna, and your buddies don't return and you don't expect them to, but the singing, the music, the smoke—they calm you and the wrinkled smile returns to your face.

There is also the smoke that gets in your eyes. You first notice it when, one day, you awaken to an empty house filled with a blue-gray haze. You dash to the kitchen, but there is no fire. You look into the corridor, but it is clear. You run to the window, but there are no fire trucks outside. And then, as you blink repeatedly, you realize that the smoke is in your eyes. Wherever you go, whatever you do, it stays with you. Washing your face doesn't help. Rubbing your eyes is just as useless. It is only when Myrtle and Edna and your buddies ask you to sing that the acrid smoke vanishes and the tears give way to smiles and shiny teeth. You realize you are in possession of still another great power and an even greater secret. "Mum is the word," says Myrtle. You nod. When Manya asks you how you spent your day, you dare not betray the others and, like that Negro who tripped over Johnny's outstretched foot, you smile.

Sometimes the smoke appears when you are outside, buying vegetables at the Market or gazing at the colorful pastries in De Roberti's window or relaxing on your favorite park bench or photographing Edna and Myrtle in front of the seesaws and swings the boy likes so much. If you stop what you are doing and hum or sing the song, the effect is always the same. The smoke rises, the contours of objects become sharper, and faces become visible. Clarity comes more quickly when you also snap your fingers. But caution is imperative. Once, you placed the pleated wire shopping basket on the floor before the smoke had fully disappeared and an Italian woman tripped and shook her umbrella at you. Another time, two men had to push you aside in order to step inside the bakery. People don't understand that, if it weren't for you, the world would remain immersed in smoke.

It's easiest to sing or hum during Sunday Mass at St. George's. You and your sisters and the boy are arrayed along a long hard bench in the balcony, just to the right of the altar and the gold-covered iconostasis with shy saints and armor-clad angels. The priest is swinging the incense holder and the sound of the lid clapping against the golden chains reminds you of castanets. As the sweetly pungent aroma fills the air, you realize the balconies are smothered

48

by smoke. It's time for action. It's time for your intervention. As the priest chants a prayer and the church choir breaks out in praising the Lord, you sing your song at the top of your voice. No one notices, except for Edna and Myrtle and the guys. Your nephew looks at you with a puzzled expression on his face and tugs on your jacket, but he says nothing and Manya and Stefa are too busy crossing themselves, genuflecting, and praying to realize you have, once again, saved the day.

Prayer comes easily to you. It always did. At home you sang in the choir and received Communion every Sunday. Father Kowcz would occasionally wonder out loud whether you shouldn't enter the seminary. You smiled, feeling flattered by his attention and expectations, all the more so as his sons were studying to become priests. Once in America, you discovered that barracks and tents were ideal places to pray, especially after lights out, when the rhythmic snoring of the men combined with the undisciplined chirping of the crickets and the rhythmic croaking of the frogs to produce the semblance of a choir. Naturally, you joined in, silently, though no less fervently than if you had been in a real church. It was then, in the darkness and amid the noise, that God sometimes appeared—very, very briefly, just long enough for you to feel a divine presence in your heart and lungs and gut.

Unfortunately, there are, increasingly, also bad days, when the viewfinder reveals evil, greed, betrayal, and guilt in the form of dangerously deranged men and women who should know better than to follow and harass you. There is the ugly old man with a gnarled cane and thick glasses who looks at you suspiciously no matter what you do. There is the slim singer in top hat and tails whose mellow voice and doe-like eyes evoke a sense of milky contentment belied by what you know are malicious intentions. There is the stately woman in tiara and mink who holds a switchblade in her hand and slides it slowly across her wrist. Who are these people? Where did they come from? And what exactly do they want from you? Did Alonzo send them? Did A.J.? You have no answers and you realize that, in threatening circumstances such as these, it's best to remove your eye from the viewfinder and to hum your song, at least until Myrtle and Edna and the gang appear and all is, once again, quite well.

Except that, sometimes, they don't appear or they take their goddam time doing so. And then you're all alone and the loneliness, vulnerability, and fear you feel are far worse than anything you experienced on the President Roosevelt way back in the fall of 1938, before any of this (of what, Mike, of what?) began and you were just a round-faced kid with a milk mustache. Why should your friends abandon you? Their callous disregard for your well-being makes no sense: they know—they *must* know—that the man with the cane, the singer in the top hat, and the stately woman in the tiara are leering at you and waiting: waiting for you to make a mistake, to trip up, to get something—anything—wrong, at which point, of course, they'll pounce and destroy you. After all, why else would they be waiting? Fortunately, Manya, Stefa, and the boy know nothing about these megalomaniacs in sheep's clothing. Neither does Manya's husband, Oleksa. It is your secret and you intend to keep it that way. They might panic and do something stupid. You've got everything under control. It's just a matter of will and vigilance, as you well know.

Manya and Stefa keep saying you should get a job. You will, you answer, no doubt about it. *But not just now.* There are other, more important, matters to be settled first. Ensuring everybody's safety is no small concern: the burden must be borne by the one man who understands the full extent of the threat. Oleksa is new to this country and speaks no English. The boy is a boy. You are the man of the house and it is your responsibility and obligation—your *sacred* responsibility and obligation—to protect the weak from the predations of the powerful. You are, you realize, in the front lines of a war: you are the only barrier between the evil that threatens to engulf the world and the innocents of the world. It goes without saying that it will be necessary to strip the stately woman of her knife.

It is impossible to say the days go by quickly, but it is equally impossible to say they go by slowly. Time appears to stand still or, perhaps more accurately, it appears to have ceased altogether, to have become obliterated and disappeared. It doesn't much matter anymore just where time is or is not experienced: the apartment, the kitchen, the toilet, the bedroom, the park, the street, the bar, the church. Time has vanished and the smoke is everywhere. Edna, Myrtle, and the guys follow you wherever you go, even when you have no camera, but so do, increasingly and worryingly, the old man, the singer, and the woman. How you long to be alone! But, whatever you do, there they are, the whole gaggle of them, an entourage fit for a king.

But you're not a king and never wanted to be one. You're just Mike, Mikey, Mikey-o, Mykhasko. Oh, how you yearn for the good ol' days of possibility! There he goes again, that Mikey-boy, snapping his fingers and shaking his head, like a really cool cat, and mumbling the words that always get the girl. Mikey-boy, hey, Mikey! Here comes a real dish, Mikey! Heck, she could be your mother. But she looks hungry, Mikey, she looks hungry and she looks like she gives. Yep, Mikey-boy, that dame looks like she gives. That dame's a tomato, Mikey-boy. Why dontcha have a bite, huh?

And then, one by one, they come to you in the night. It might be in your dreams or it might not. They are too real to be dreams, but they are also too evanescent to be fully real. They stand at your bed, whispering and laughing and drinking cocktails. Sometimes they snap their fingers and drop coins into a jukebox. Sometimes the old man glowers, while the crooner and the stately woman shuffle their feet as they do the jitterbug. Sometimes you see the knife glowing like a candle in her hand. Once Edna tried to get into bed with you, but you pushed her away and she cried bitterly. Another time, it was Myrtle, but you reminded her of Alonzo and she withdrew. And, still another time, the stately woman climbed atop your loins with the knife between her teeth. You shoved her away with all your might and she tumbled to the floor and lay there, giggling, as you awoke and ran your hand across your wet brow. The knife, you remind yourself, I have to take the knife from her.

One day, you do just that. You are sitting in the kitchen and there, right before you, lies the switchblade. You make a grab for it just as the woman extends her hand. Both of you are holding the handle and you are surprised by her strength. She looks you in the eyes, daring you to overcome her and knowing you cannot. You jerk your hand to the left and, unexpectedly, free the knife from her iron grip. She jumps from her seat, ready to pounce, while you lash out, stabbing and cutting and stabbing and cutting until she is on the floor, covered in blood, her clothes disheveled, her coiffeur fatally disturbed. Overwhelmed by the fatal battle you've just fought, you faint and fall to the cracked and faded green linoleum, where you lie next to her motionless body.

When Manya finds you, you explain that your wounds were incurred in a great struggle with a woman who wears a tiara and resembles the Queen and carries a knife, but that you defended yourself ably and that all is OK: there is absolutely nothing for her and Stefa to worry about. We are all safe, you cry, perfectly safe. Your sister looks unpersuaded and you realize she may have a point. The bitch just might decide to come back. The hag could've crawled off somewhere. She might very well be licking her wounds and planning to return and resume her sinister campaign. "But don't worry, Manya, don't worry, I'll be prepared this time, I'll be fully prepared."

Manya shakes her head silently as she cleans your wounds, but she obviously understands her little brother. As does Stefa. All is well. The only thing to worry about is the form and timing of the next attack, which is inevitable. The woman who resembles the Queen won't use a knife again: that would be too obvious. Of course! She'll use stealth; she'll use poison. And where better to introduce it than into the food: the borscht, the cabbage soup, the potato dumplings, the sour cream, the fried onions, the walnut cakes, donuts, the scrambled eggs? Very well, if that's her strategy, you'll be on full alert. Her poison can't work if you refuse to eat.

And if the old man with the cane and the bald crooner try something, you'll be prepared for them, too. Should Edna and Myrtle and the boys be warned? Yes, they should ready themselves as well. Best to do it by means of the radio, in code. The enemy is everywhere, after all, and he—or she!—can strike anytime and anywhere. Thank God for your training in the army.

Edna is behaving oddly, almost crazily, and you are worried. While the others are smiling or laughing or dancing or snapping their fingers, she stands quietly at the bar, dabbing her eyes with a handkerchief and taking quick, short gulps from the cocktail glass. Every once in a while, she peers at you from beneath her brow with what appears to be anger or revulsion or contempt and you feel an icy chill run up and down your spine. This is all wrong. Edna is your girl. She loves you. She said so herself. Can she have forgotten all the good times you had? The boys used to say, "Careful, Mike, there ain't nothing worse than a gal's been dumped." They said she'd want her revenge, for sure. "She'll scratch your eyes out, Mikey, if you let her too close." But California is three thousand miles from New York and, besides, Edna is dead. There is nothing to fear.

Except, of course, that there is. Without warning, Edna starts visiting you every night. She tells you things you'd prefer not to know and not to hear: how she loved you more than anything, even more than herself, how you had no right to leave her when she gave you the best years of her life, how she told you she'd do something drastic if you left, how it was you, Mike, you and only you who killed her. "Why don't you come to me, Mike? It's easy. Just take the knife. Or take some sleeping pills, like I did. Or climb to the roof, look down at the kids playing stickball in the street below, and take one little step forward. It's easy, Mike. If I could do it, you can do it."

One day, as you are sitting in your room, deciphering the codes being transmitted on the radio and assessing your increasingly dire circumstances, it strikes you with the force of a jackhammer: Edna must be behind the gnawing unease, the constriction in your chest, the threats! How obvious. Indeed, it is so obvious that it's no wonder you hadn't realized it until now. She is pretending to be on my side, but in reality she's betrayed me. She's taking her revenge by joining forces with the ugly old man, the effeminate crooner, and the pretentious woman. You can't blame her, of course, but the betrayal is painful nonetheless. On the other hand, at least there is less guilt. And who knows? Perhaps all the guilt will evaporate if you submit to her will?

There is no memory and no experience of anything after March of 1951, when Oleksa and your veteran buddies escort you to Bellevue. (Did you go willingly, Mike, or did you resist? Did you know where they were taking you? Did you suspect you'd never return to the land of the living?) And that void lasts until the very end; indeed, it continues after your end. There is nothing. You are in some ward, you undergo electric shock therapy, you become a chain smoker, you are usually calm when your sisters and their husbands visit you, you enjoy the potato dumplings and stuffed cabbage rolls they bring, and then you die—from some illness, from old age, from futility. There is nothing more to say. For a brief time, you enjoyed expansiveness and possibility. Life was a train sailing along the steppes. And then the walls came in on you and the lights were turned off.

The King's Park hospital grounds on Long Island are full of luxuriant trees and neatly trimmed hedges and even the sky above can be an azure blue in the summer, but I doubt you ever noticed or cared. I doubt that Myrtle or Edna or A.J. or the boys or the old man or the crooner or the stately woman ever visited you. Besides, the men in white took your camera away and severed your only connection to the past, the present, and the future. All that remains of you is, not the memory, because there is none, nor the click-click-clicking, because it ceased decades ago, but a flag folded into a tight triangle and a white slab inscribed with your name among thousands of identical stones inscribed with other names.

Chapter 2
Manya

The eyes closed permanently on Tuesday evening, but the breathing continued until Saturday afternoon, when, after several mighty inhalations through the withered mouth, it ceased. And that was the end, almost exactly as I had wished it. I had always prayed I would fall asleep one night and never awaken. There was at first a fever and my breathing became labored, but the fever subsided within a day or two and the breathing resumed its normal rhythm. For more than two days, I lay quietly in my own bed, inhaling through my nose and exhaling through my mouth, occasionally moving a finger or a toe, but otherwise remaining quite still, as if I were indeed asleep. And then, on Saturday, a little after noon, my inhalations and exhalations became faster and shorter, until, just before the end, they slowed down and, just before the very end, for no more than a few minutes, maybe thirty at the most, I breathed through my mouth, almost as if I were hoping to suck in as much life as I possibly could before embarking on my final journey. There followed in rapid succession three or four deep inhalations and it was over.

There was so much life before that end, but there was also death at the beginning. I was eight or nine, Mike was three, and Stefa had just been born. Mama fell ill and, after a few days in the hospital and after the large mirror in our living room crashed in the middle of the night, she breathed her last breath, eighty-nine years before I breathed mine. We knew that, when mirrors fall to the floor for no reason and break into millions of shards, bad things always happen and bad things did happen.

It was wintertime. We drove to the cemetery on a plain wooden cart led by two shivering horses: it snowed and an icy wind blew and I had to wrap myself tightly in my coat. Mike held me by the waist for warmth and comfort and we almost froze by the time we got there. It was a big cemetery, just across the street from a brown church with one lonely spire. The somber-looking men carried Mama's coffin through the iron gate, past the naked trees, and toward an empty field in the back, where they lowered it into a big hole—I remember thinking I had never seen such a big hole—and said some prayers and sang some sad songs. Everybody wept and then they filled the hole with clumps of frozen soil—the shovels made a scratchy noise and the earth pummeled the coffin like hail—and we returned in the same cart amid the same snow and icy wind. My godparents kissed me on the forehead and embraced Tato, who was crying. My father never cried, but I could see him rubbing his eyes with the back of his shoemaker's hand and breathing very hard. Mike cried, too, although I'm not sure he knew just why.

I tried to hold back my tears, but they came anyway, though not as hard as the day we learned Mama was no more. That was a shock. I couldn't believe it and I couldn't understand it. Some of our neighbors had died, but this, when your own mother died, was different. Would I never see her again? Not here, they said, but in Heaven. That was good news and I knew it anyway from school, but not to be able to see and feel and hear Mama, *here*, right here in our warm house on Division Street, that was something I couldn't quite grasp. Who would bake those delicious cakes and donuts? Who would give me a penny to buy potato chips from the little Portuguese man at the foot of the street? Who would walk me to school and kiss me on the head before the girls' entrance? Who would take me to the shore and collect snails in a small pail and boil and serve them as dinner and show us how to extract them with sewing pins? Who would laugh at Mike as he screwed up his face at the sight of the squiggly, gray things? I soon learned that no one would. It was as simple as that. That was my first encounter with death and its impossible finality. It wouldn't be my last.

We lived at the bottom of a steep hill, on this side of a railroad track and train depot that separated the houses from the motionless water of the metallic bay and the narrow, pebble-stoned beach where we went swimming. Boxy, white, wooden clapboard houses, four or five stories tall, lined most of the street. It was only on our block that the houses were small and had large green yards where the stout Portuguese women planted vines and tomatoes and, together with their wiry cigarette-smoking husbands, sat in the summer drinking wine and roasting fish, while their children played on the grass. Long undulating lines of colorful laundry—bed sheets, towels, shirts, socks, underwear, and scores of diapers—crisscrossed the cavernous spaces, flapping in the breeze that came from the bay, turning a bright hard white in the summer and emitting steam, almost as if they were on fire, in the winter.

Our house was brown, with a slanted roof, an attic, a coal-burning stove, and a room facing the street that served as Tato's workshop. He made, fixed, and polished shoes in a tiny space that was lined with all kinds of leathers, smelly glues, hammers, knives, and jars of nails. The Portuguese and Irish and our people, too, all came to Tato with their dirty, old, beat-up shoes and, after a few hours in his care, they'd come out looking brand new, clean and smooth and straight with hard tan soles and black heels that reminded me of little candy boxes. We lived well. There was always food on the table, sometimes even bananas and chocolate, and I had a few dresses, blouses, skirts, and a nice coat with large shiny buttons. And, naturally, Stefa, Mike, and I always had the best shoes around. No kids could compete with us, because their fathers worked in the textile mills and sometimes came home without fingers, while our Tato made the best shoes in Fall River. His closest friends, our godfathers, also worked as shoemakers.

The Catholic school was about five blocks up the hill. Every morning, Mama would take me by the hand and, just before we reached the squat, red-brick building, she'd buy me a sweet bun in the Portuguese bakery on the corner and the owner would look at my black hair and olive skin and say to Mama, "She looks like one of us, Missus Annie. You sure you ain't Portuguese?" From there you could actually see the bay down below and the park to the left and the factories with their mighty smokestacks to the right. On some days the clouds and the smoke seemed to fuse and I couldn't tell where one ended and the other began, but it didn't matter, since I had the bun and could feel its soft warmth in the palm of my hand. Mama always said I should learn to read and write, because that was important in today's world. She said she couldn't even read a newspaper or sign her name properly. She could, as a matter of fact, but very slowly and with great effort, almost as if she had memorized the signature and was trying to remember how to draw the squiggles.

And then there was the park, the great, big, rolling, green park, where we ran and played, while Stefa watched from the blanket, where she crawled about or just sat and made a mess of some cookie. Mike and I would roll down the hill, tumbling over and over, and the leaves and the grass would stick to our hair and clothes and leave stains that Mama would wash out with a smelly yellow soap. And sometimes I'd take Mike all the way down: we'd cross a bridge and watch the trains roll along below and run to the beach, where we'd take off our shoes and, oohing and aahing as we ran across the hard pebbles, step into the cool waters of the bay. I'd hold Mike's hand and say, "This is Narragansett Bay, Mykhasko." And he'd try to repeat the words and say "Narransett" and I'd laugh and laugh until my belly ached. Then I'd suddenly remember that Mama was expecting us with sandwiches and cocoa and we'd put on our shoes and run back up the hill. Mike's face would be as red as a lobster when we finally arrived and Mama said, "Now sit down and eat."

Our idyllic existence ended when Mama died and our lives came crashing down like the mirror in the living room. Mama was dead and Tato must have figured there was no earthly reason for us to stay in Fall River, not with three children and an empty, silent house and a delicious garden that needed tending and no wife. Tato told us Mama's last wish was that he take her children back home, that they not grow up among foreigners, not when they had no mother to take care of them. So it was in the spring of 1923 that he sold the furniture, the house, and his shoemaking things—the leather and scissors and knives and glues and dyes and waxes and nails and threads—and left the rest to my godparents and packed our clothes in three large trunks with tan leather straps. When he finished, he looked at the cases and said, "That's it, Manya, that's our whole life."

We took a train to New York City and, after we arrived at what looked to me like the largest and busiest train station in the world, he hired a man with a tired-looking horse and cart to take us to a pier where we crawled up a long and wobbly ramp hanging precariously above the swirling dirty water below. Once we got to the top, we were on a ship, a very big ship that crossed the ocean to Hamburg, Germany, which I knew was in a faraway continent called Europe. I don't remember exactly how long the trip took, but I do remember how the Statue of Liberty, which, to my great surprise, was a sickly pale green, grew smaller and smaller until it disappeared. Then the shoreline and the lights disappeared and then there was nothing, absolutely nothing but froth-edged waves and graveyard sky with thick clouds and jagged lightning bolts that appeared silently amid the impenetrable blackness of the liquid night.

I slept in an upper berth, as did Mike, while Tato and Stefa, who cried a lot, slept below. I read my books and played with Mike and Stefa and, when people asked Tato who he was and why he was traveling with three little children (or "childs," as he used to say) and I could see he didn't understand, I would translate for him or even answer on my own. The food was terrible and, every time I swallowed a spoonful of the porridge or potato soup or bit into the tasteless white bread, I thought of Mama and her wonderful cakes and rolls and chicken. I cried, but only a little, as Mike and Stefa had to be fed, cleaned, or tended to and there wasn't any time to feel too sad or too preoccupied with my own worries.

One night, an immense storm tossed the ship and pounded its sides like a drum. None of us could sleep. Stefa, as usual, was crying and Mike was whimpering, so I climbed down and Tato and I took them in our arms and we sang the songs Mama used to sing when she cooked or baked or cleaned the house. Stefa and Mike quickly fell asleep and Tato said I should go back to my berth, but I whispered, "I'll stay and help you," and he squeezed my hand and kissed my forehead. That's where he always kissed me, on the forehead, while Mama mostly kissed me on the cheeks, sometimes on the left one, sometimes on the right one, and sometimes on both, back and forth, back and forth, until it tickled unbearably and I squealed and escaped her embrace.

And then, one day, we emerged from the milky-white opaqueness and pulled into Hamburg. Lazy gulls circled the ship and weather-beaten sailors pulled on ropes and shouted in German. The port smelled of rotten fish. Fortunately, we soon boarded a train to Lviv, where some man whom Tato embraced tightly loaded our things on a cart and took us to Przemyślany, a name that struck me as needlessly complicated and far less appealing than Fall River. Our new home was made of brick and plaster and it was about as large as our old house. Everything else was different. Przemyślany had one main street; Fall River had many. Fall River had a huge bay; Przemyślany had a small stream. Fall River had a magnificent park; Przemyślany had wheat fields and forests. No one spoke English in Przemyślany, but everyone spoke Polish, Yiddish, or Ukrainian. And I quickly learned I had more relatives than I could ever have imagined. In Fall River it was just the five of us and our godparents. Here there were uncles and aunts and cousins and grandparents: some were Ukrainian and some were Polish, but they all spoke both languages and constantly visited one another.

There were many more relatives in the cemetery up the hill. Mama should have been buried there and it saddened me to think that she lay in some corner of a small graveyard thousands of miles away, that I would never again see the spot where she rested beneath the grass, and that my mental picture of the strong woman who gave me life and weaned me and taught me how to cook and clean and take care of my siblings and my father would fade like a colorful scarf after too many washings. We visited the cemetery often, to lay flowers, to tend to the graves, and there was sometimes singing, the burning of incense, and the holding upright of heavy blue and gold flags. But it was always my mother I thought of when I entered the grounds of the dead. She was gone. She had left my life as fully and completely as one possibly can. But I still felt her all around me. I sensed her soul hovering above me and I saw her smile in the trees, wind, grass, and poppies. And when we stood before some grave and prayed or sang, it was Mama's grave I was standing before. I think Tato felt the same way. He'd grow unusually pensive in the cemetery and his gaze would wander, from the crowd or the grave to some point in the distance, beyond the trees, beyond the horizon—to Fall River, of course.

We lived with my grandmother, Tato's mother, a near-toothless old woman with a beak-like nose and soft eyes who always wore a dark kerchief tightly bundled around her small, bird-like head. She had bought the house with the money Tato sent her from America. Although she could count on me to help with chores, I could see she'd never manage with the three of us. Tato had no choice and, just a few months after we arrived in Przemyślany, took a new wife. Her name was Anastasia and she was a widow and it was rumored that Tato had known her when he was still young. We called her Mama, except that I knew she wasn't, not really, and never would or could be. After all, a mother can never be replaced.

Stefa couldn't remember our dead mother and Mike quickly forgot the woman who lay in the North Burial Ground. They grew accustomed to the new Mama's presence in our house. But not me.

It was our house, just as the brown house in Fall River was ours. How could I get used to her, especially as I could still see my real mother so vividly? It wasn't just the images I remembered. It was also the smells, maybe most of all the smells: her cooking, the house, and her body: her bosom, her arms, her neck, and her luxuriant hair. The reassuring smell of her firm flesh stayed with me all the time, even on the ship, amid the salt water and the putrid odor of the other passengers and the dull, unwashed stench of the bed sheets, mattresses, and pillows.

Tato and my stepmother soon had three more children and, by the end of the 1920s, when I was about fifteen or sixteen, there were nine of us children in a house built for far fewer. We slept all over the place, in the bedroom, in the living room, in the kitchen, on beds, on cots, on benches, and, during the summer, even on the floor or in the garden. I'm not sure our stepmother disliked Stefa, Mike, and me, but she favored her own offspring over us. I could cope, even with the complete lack of privacy, but Stefa and Mike couldn't understand just why they always had less to eat or why their socks had holes or why their shoes were too tight or too old or had no shoelaces and had to be tied with bits of old string.

With nine children and one wage, Tato was unable to afford much of anything. I had one nice dress, one skirt, two blouses, one slip, two pairs of socks, and two pairs of underwear. Our material circumstances were unenviable, to say the least, but they never interfered with our cleanliness. Stefa, Mike, and I would go to the public baths behind the synagogue every Saturday and scrub ourselves with pumice until our skin turned red and we'd wash our hair with the tan soap our stepmother used to clean especially greasy dishes, pots, and pans.

Fortunately, there was school. I learned well and my grades were good enough to get me admitted into the Queen Jadwiga Coeducational Gymnasium. Tato was terribly proud, even though he could barely pay the tuition with the meager income he collected tilling some land and repairing the occasional shoe. The gymnasium gave me a good education, of course, but it also gave me my two best friends, Mańka and Fanka. Mańka was Polish and she lived across the street from Ss. Peter and Paul Catholic Church in the center of town. Her father was assistant director of the post office. Fanka was Jewish and her father was a prosperous local merchant; her family inhabited a beautiful villa off the main street named after Poland's national poet, Adam Mickiewicz. The three of us sang in the school choir and we often performed on stage during national holidays. The Principal even gave us lavish rose bouquets after our rendition of the Polish national anthem brought the audience to tears on Independence Day. When we donned our Sunday best and paraded through town, we knew we'd always be treated to sweets. We were Mańka, Fanka, and Manya and we were inseparable—until, of course, two invasions and a war separated us forever.

Mańka was the coquette all the boys adored. She'd bestow a regal smile on some favorite and he'd immediately take to opening doors, bringing flowers, and offering his arm. Fanka was the artist. She dressed elegantly, was exceptionally well-read, and played the piano with genuine feeling. But flirting was not for her. When she first saw Vlodko, I could see from the dazed expression on her face that she had fallen in love. "Go ahead, you silly goose!" Mańka would say. "Smile at him." But Fanka never did: at most, she'd steal a glance, lock her eyes to his for a brief second, and then hurriedly turn away.

Then, one day in the late spring, the boys invited us for ice cream. Without saying a word, Vlodko took Fanka by the arm and led her to the sweets shop where we sat at a long table near the window and laughed and told jokes and gossiped about our teachers and watched the people walk by. "He's in the Organization of Ukrainian Nationalists," I told Fanka next day. "So what?" she said indifferently. "They could arrest him any day." "It doesn't matter," she replied. "I'll wait for him as long as I have to."

Fanka's large eyes and long eyelashes perfectly complemented her oval face, gently uplifted nose, and kind mouth. Vlodko was as handsome as she was pretty: jet black hair combed straight back, an authoritative mustache, and glowing eyes suggested a severity in his demeanor that did not quite correspond to the reality. He was serious—especially about the things he loved: Fanka and his country—but beneath that seriousness lay a sensitive personality that verged on shyness. When, during the war, he preferred suicide to capture by the Soviet secret police, I was shocked, but not surprised.

I always knew his patriotism would get him into trouble. The authorities were constantly harassing the nationalists, especially after one of them assassinated some minister in 1934 and the trial that followed generated enormous excitement among the young. My male friends adopted an exaggerated swagger, almost as if they wanted to provoke a fight with the Poles, who were just as eager to show them who was in charge. Vlodko wasn't among the brawlers, but his pride was unmistakable. Fanka shared that pride. The other Jewish girls kept to themselves or were only friends with the Polish students; Fanka actually preferred the company of the tiny Ukrainian minority to her own kind. We admired and loved her even more for her courage.

Like Fanka, I, too, met the love of my life: a dashing boy who stole and broke my heart. Stefan was taller than most of the others. Like Vlodko's, his black hair was combed back; when it stayed in place, it revealed a prominent forehead and a perfectly straight nose that was nestled between darkly languorous eyes suspended beneath gently curved eyebrows and resting on sculpted cheeks held together by a perfect mouth. Stefan was beautiful and he dressed accordingly. His fedora was set at a rakish angle over his eyes, his long coat flowed majestically like a king's robe, and his tie was always slightly uncentered, creating the impression of devil-may-care indifference to a beauty he knew he possessed in spades. When I put on my finest, we turned heads as we promenaded about town.

Unfortunately, we fought constantly about the littlest and stupidest of things. Was the battle of wills due to his looks and my jealousy? Or was it due to my force of character and his weakness? Because jealous I was. Who wouldn't be, when the heads that turned were as often those of girls as of boys? And weak he was, too. Stefan needed to be coddled, mothered, and reassured he was the only one I could ever love. I was happy to oblige, but at some point his insecurity would annoy me—as perhaps mine did him—and I'd make a cutting remark I'd immediately regret.

The turbulence might have passed had it not been for his wandering eye. Let him look, I told myself at first: that's perfectly fine and all men do it. But when Stefan started seeing other girls behind my back, I put my foot down and gave him an ultimatum. He vowed to be faithful, but I knew his promises were empty and I was right. Within a week of making a promise, he'd be breaking it and always with someone new. Finally, I said good-bye. He pleaded and assured me he would change, but I said enough is enough: we were over and I never wanted to see him again. That was in 1939, a few months before the communists invaded and our whole world ended.

We barely saw each other during the war. He eventually married a vivacious blonde I never liked and it was clear within a few weeks that the marriage was a failure. Stefan took to arranging seemingly accidental meetings with me, during which he'd beg me to take him back. "Take you back?" I hissed. "You're married. Go home to your wife." As he fell silent, I could see his eyes moisten and I thought: Why didn't you cry when we were a couple? Why couldn't you let me see your gentle side? Why did you always argue? I'm sure I was no angel, but it was your betrayals, Stefan, that brought you and me to this unhappy end.

Alas, Stefan's end was especially unhappy. A daughter was born in 1944, just before I left for the west. One year later, she died and then he died. I learned of his death a few years later, when I was already in America. He contracted tuberculosis, his condition worsened, and, as he lay dying, he apparently kept repeating my name. Would he have still been alive if I hadn't left? Would he have still been alive if we hadn't quarreled? His wife felt insulted by his last words and, after burying him in the cemetery and planting a simple iron cross above him and their daughter, she left town. And that's all that's left of my beautiful Stefan: an iron cross tucked away in the back of an obscure provincial graveyard.

That and a few photographs. There is one of him in his trademark fedora and long gray coat with his dandy's eyes peering out from beneath the tilted rim. He is walking, one foot is extended, his hands are in his pockets, and the buttons on his coat are shining. There is another of him in a jacket and tie, his hands on his hips, laughing, his head turned slightly to the left, his neck muscles tensed, his hair just slightly tousled. And there is one of me and him. I am standing in a doorway, a dark hat set over my eyes, no smile on my face, with my gloved hands perched on his shoulders. He is wearing his fedora, scarf, and coat and is standing as if I were not there. We are looking in different directions, almost as if we suspected that the future had no place for us.

There have been too many deaths, far too many deaths, and I am not sure I know, or ever knew, how to cope with them. How can a child survive the death of its mother? How can a girl live after her beloved turns to dirt? And there were so many more, far too many, far more than anyone can possibly imagine or survive. Is it any wonder we are all crippled by life?

After I graduated from Queen Jadwiga's in 1937 and began giving private lessons, my father's sister, Kateryna (or Ciocia Kaśka as we used to call her) said I could live with her family—she had married a Polish court clerk, Jan, and they had four sons—in their spacious new house. How could I refuse my very own room? I immediately said yes, knowing Tato would be delighted and my stepmother relieved to have one less mouth to feed. I still recall the exquisite pleasure I felt the first night I lay in bed and pulled the covers over my eyes. I was back on Division Street. I was a little girl again: Mama was asleep in an adjoining room and all would be well. She would never die and no one, absolutely no one, would ever die. I remember thinking that all one needed to make life wonderful was a little bed you could call your own—and, if possible, a mother who would kiss you on the forehead before saying goodnight and tuck you in. And then my flight of fancy came crashing to the earth: there was no mother. Mama lay dead in Fall River and there wasn't even a rusty iron cross to mark the spot.

And then there came another death, even if a metaphorical one. My little brother left for the United States in late 1938. After finishing grade school, he started working in a grocery store as a low-paid assistant. The Polish authorities insisted Mike give up his American citizenship before he could qualify for a decent job. He refused. Tato and I agreed he had done the right thing, but we also realized that his refusal meant there was no longer any reason for him to stay in Przemyślany and every reason to return to America. After Mike got the necessary papers from the U.S. Embassy in Warsaw, my father and I pooled our savings and bought him a ticket on a ship bound for New York: the President Roosevelt.

We escorted my little brother to the train station: never again would he see the glorious linden trees lining that leafy road. We waited almost an hour on the platform and then, almost unexpectedly, the terrible moment arrived and the train appeared on the horizon, blew its whistle, and neared the station. The steam rose like a morning mist from beneath the carriage, while the conductors jumped to the ground and called on the passengers to show their tickets and take their seats. I embraced Mykhasko one last time. I felt his warm tears on my right cheek as he was torn from me and pushed up the stairs, a look of confusion, fear, consternation, and indifference on his moon-like face. He stood at the window with the palms of both hands pressed against the pane. When the train began moving, the glare from the sun obliterated his image and all we could do was blow kisses and wave our handkerchiefs and point at the window behind which he presumably still stood, crushed and saddened and terrified by the great journey he was about to undertake. I went home to Ciocia Kaśka's that night and ran to my room and cried. Would I ever see my little brother again? I would, of course, though I couldn't have known that then. Nor could I have known we'd never resume a normal life together. Mike would die for me a second time and that second death would be far more painful than the first, almost as painful as Mama's.

After Mike left for America and the fog of despair had lifted, I resolved to be sensible and follow his example. There was no reason to stay: Stefan was gone, I had no hope of getting a job as long as I clung to my American passport, and even a fool could see that Europe was headed toward a cataclysm. I was booked on a ship from Bremen to New York for mid-October 1939; I had even begun to clean out my personal things. And then, on September 1, Germany attacked Poland and we cheered, until we learned that our stepmother's brother had been killed on the front. "War is a terrible thing," Tato said sorrowfully. "I lost three brothers in Bosnia in the first days of the last war. I would probably have been killed as well, if I hadn't immigrated to America in 1913."

A little more than two weeks later, the Russians invaded what was left of Poland and my world collapsed once again. I was walking along Mickiewicz Street when a winding column of Soviet tanks appeared at the top of the hill near the cemetery and thundered toward me. I was transfixed by the noise and dust and power. We humans were nothing compared to these steel monsters. They could smash and devour us and all we could do was accept our tragic end. But I also felt confused. The soldiers spoke a soft Ukrainian and sang haunting folk songs and said they were liberating us from the oppression of Polish landlord rule. The Poles stayed indoors, but the Jews and Ukrainians went into the streets and waved and laughed and looked at one another knowingly, as if they had expected no less from the Russians all along. Some Ukrainians gave the soldiers bread and salt, some Jews rushed to the tanks and kissed them. Almost overnight, we had become part of the proletarian paradise, the Soviet Union, and my trip to America had been cancelled.

Stunned, I unpacked my things, carefully returned my personal items to the higher shelves and drawers, and tried to reconcile myself to the sudden turn in my fate. At first, the future looked promising. Our "liberators" and overlords held elections and we were actually encouraged to vote. The outcome was abundantly clear—unification with Soviet Ukraine was preordained—but the fanfare surrounding the process pleased everybody. Jews and Ukrainians got good jobs—I became a secretary in the regional cooperative—while, overnight, Poles were reduced to what we had been before the invasion: second-class citizens. We felt sorry for our relatives, but who could complain about our enhanced status after so many years of maltreatment by the Polish authorities? Our Jewish neighbors on Pocztowa were particularly enthusiastic about Soviet rule: most were poor and their status as "proletarians" immediately granted them hitherto unimaginable privileges. Everyone noticed the change in their bearing. Tirkisz became insufferable, accusing Tato of insufficient loyalty to the new regime. Jenta began speaking a broken form of Russian and regarded any salutations in Ukrainian with a scowl. Moszko the barber placed a large portrait of Stalin in his store window.

Very quickly, however, the Bolsheviks showed their true colors. All our institutions, from parties to choirs to clubs to the church, were either shut down or placed under official control. Community life came to a standstill. Red flags, posters of the great Stalin, and the hammer and sickle came to adorn all public buildings. In the first half of 1940, prominent Poles, Jews, and Ukrainians vanished in several waves of arrests and deportations. I knew many of them personally. A few months later their families were herded into battered cattle cars and the trains disappeared over the horizon to the east—to Kazakhstan. We never heard from any of them again. No one—not a single Pole, Jew, or Ukrainian—dared protest publicly, since we all knew that such recklessness would get us arrested or deported or even killed. People counted their blessings, thankful that someone else, and not they, had met so sad a fate. Privately, we were outraged and cursed the Russians. But we learned to be cautious: you never knew who might denounce you to the police. The fear and suspicion ultimately became intolerable. The only good that came of these black months is that the Polish and Ukrainian sides of our family found a common bond in hatred of the Russian occupiers.

Despite their brutality, many people remained loyal to them. Little Ivanko, the son of a distinguished Ukrainian doctor, joined the Komsomol, became an enthusiastic informer, and denounced scores of patriots to the secret police. He became the terror of the town. Tirkisz, Jenta, and many of the recent refugees from Hitler's half of Poland continued to support the regime even after the deportations, perhaps because some of the most visible local Soviet officials were Jews. People couldn't fail to notice. They eyed their Jewish neighbors with fear and avoided meeting or conversing with them. They might inform on you. They might take their personal revenge on you for some earlier slight. Who knew? It seemed best to ignore them or to greet them fleetingly and walk past in silence, with your head bowed low and your breathing hushed.

The Bolsheviks had made our life unlivable. For all its many faults, Poland now seemed like a paradise. We had been able to speak, live, and think more or less freely. There had been spies and informers, but they had only spied and informed on the nationalists. In contrast, life under the Bolsheviks had become a hell for everyone. We were constantly afraid, constantly looking over our shoulders, constantly suspicious. The tension was unbearable, except that we had no choice but to bear it—a state of affairs that, I'm tempted to say, applies to life in general. By 1941 my nationalist friends were talking about going underground and starting a resistance movement. Others fled west to Kraków. There were rumors of an impending German attack on the Soviet Union, but no one believed them. After all, the Soviet press fawned over Hitler and Nazi Germany on a daily basis. Why should two close friends become enemies?

At the same time, life went on, as it always does. I'd learned that in Fall River, even if half-consciously, and I was learning it all over again in Przemyślany. People die, cataclysms strike, wars erupt,

70

families collapse, but the survivors always manage to continue living, even when it seems as if there's no point in doing so. And so we lived. The red flags kept flying, Stalin kept smiling cynically at us from every wall, and arrests and disappearances kept taking place with terrible ferocity, while we continued sleeping, waking, bathing, working, cooking, eating, laughing, flirting, and crying. People are people and they remain people even when conditions force them to behave as beasts. I still lived at Ciocia Kaśka's and I still met with Mańka—Fanka, by then, was already studying piano at the Lviv Conservatory—and we still walked along Mickiewicz Street and the boys still invited us for coffee or ice cream at the *cukernia* and the entire family still met on name days and holidays and holydays and sang songs and went on picnics and exchanged gifts. Life may be harder to live during wars and occupations, but it still has to be lived—and is lived.

Mike kept in touch sporadically. Although he tried to put on a brave face in his letters, it was clear from reading between the lines that his first few months in New York had been exceptionally difficult and that he was having serious doubts about his decision to emigrate. Sometime in early 1939, he informed us he'd signed up for a government program for unemployed young men and would be shipped out west, to the mountains and forests, and that he probably wouldn't have time to write as often as he'd like to— which, of course, was very little anyway. The news of his impending journey saddened me greatly. My little brother would be several thousand kilometers farther away. He was already half way around the world, so that additional distance shouldn't have mattered, but it seemed to me that fate was taking him away just as I was planning to join him.

What was I to do in Przemyślany? Mike was gone. Mańka was engaged to one of her suitors. Fanka was in Lviv. Stefa was there, too, living with some seamstress and serving as her apprentice. Stefan was chasing his women. My father was trying to make ends meet and growing whiter by the day. And my mother lay in some cemetery in Fall River in an unmarked grave. When the Germans and Russians divided Poland, they settled my fate. It was a shock and a tragedy and I was bitter for days. And then I realized: we are all prisoners of our fates. We think we live freely, but the reality is that life makes our choices for us. Sometimes it makes good choices and we think we are happy and in control and sometimes it makes bad choices and we think we are sad and powerless. Ultimately, however, we are just pawns and pawns have no choice but to place their fate in God's strong hands.

How was Mike coping with the Rocky Mountains? It was hard to imagine my chubby little brother swinging an axe and felling towering fir trees. And it was impossible to believe that this hesitant boy was becoming a young man. Did he have a girl? Did he have friends? Who sewed on his buttons or mended his socks? Who cut his toenails? Was he warm? I imagined the American West as a cold, harsh place full of wolves, bears, and other wild animals hunted by red-skinned Indians with bows and arrows. And there, amid this savage wilderness, was a vulnerable camp with drafty wooden barracks and rickety cots full of lice-infested young Americans, who never bathed, always chewed gum, and constantly made wisecracks. How could my little Mykhasko cope with them? How could he survive? And then I'd remind myself that, however dismal his circumstances seemed to be, they couldn't possibly be worse than what was transpiring around us. Mike wasn't political. He didn't belong to the nationalists. But the NKVD was undiscriminating. It arrested anybody it suspected and it could just as easily have arrested a clumsy boy as a hardened patriot.

I did run into Vlodko occasionally, but only when visiting friends. He was keeping a low profile and tried to avoid public events, which attracted secret police spies. Fanka was well, he said, still studying piano, although she was courting danger by openly criticizing the atheism of the regime. He visited Lviv as often as he could, but the trains were dangerous and the roads were patrolled;

he preferred to go by night, crouching in the back of some horse-drawn cart or walking. Lviv was bursting with NKVD agents and Red Army soldiers, so he'd arrange to meet with Fanka in cemeteries, usually near the monument of some Polish poet. They walked the winding paths and held hands and exchanged glances and spoke in whispers. I couldn't help but smile at the image of Fanka and Vlodko surrounded by moldy statues of angels, muses, heroes, and literati, but I also shuddered at what I hoped wasn't a foreboding. Death always followed me and those I loved. Why should it stop at, of all places, the gates of a graveyard?

They summoned me to secret-police headquarters several times, hoping to convince me to abandon my American passport and become a citizen of the great Soviet state. They badgered and cajoled me, usually in Russian, and mustered every possible argument—I could study at a university, I could join the Party, my family's material circumstances would improve immediately—but theirs was a lost cause. I'd never agree to serve a godless government that was systematically destroying my culture. So I listened quietly, smiling demurely and declining on the grounds that my little brother was in America and I had to retain this one remaining connection to him. And besides, I said, I was fed up with studying and had no political aspirations and my family was getting by well enough.

At the end of my last visit they mentioned Stefa and her fiancé, a young nationalist from Zbaraż by the name of Bohdan. "You may want to warn your sister about her liaisons," the stony-faced Colonel Berman, his chest bursting with medals, said. "We know who he is and we have our eye on him." Terrified, I ran home and told Stefa, but she laughed off the threat, saying her Bohdan was anything but foolhardy. "Don't worry," she said. "I've got everything under control." But did she? She was nineteen and naïve and thought she understood the world. And she was headstrong—like my mother, I suppose. She and Bohdan paid a high price for her stubbornness, just a few months after their wedding, an all-too-briefly joyous occasion presided over by Father Kowcz. For a few hours, all of us could bask in their happiness and pretend the demons outside had no fangs and did not exist.

What struck us most about the Russians was their lack of rudimentary manners. We were shocked to see their wives wear slips or nightgowns in the street. Evidently, they had never seen such dainty garments and, having no qualms about donning the attire of the dead and deported, assumed they must be expensive evening dresses. Had they no consciences? Had they no sense of right or wrong or, at least, of good taste and good manners? Obviously not. The officers reeked of alcohol and garlic, scratched their private parts in public, and went about town burping loudly or producing other bodily sounds. Worst of all were the secret policemen. They leered at the girls, made crude remarks, and were quick to use a cudgel or a knife to force confessions from those poor souls who had the misfortune to fall into their hands. We ran when we saw them and prayed to God they hadn't seen us. The contrast with the Polish authorities couldn't have been greater. The Poles, too, could be brutes. They, too, tortured and beat our young men and women. But they always retained some measure of civility. They always smiled and spoke politely. I suppose their refinement made no difference to the poor prisoners. Still, Polish policemen didn't make you feel like dogs. The Russians did. But we learned to live with that, too. We had learned to live with every indignity and atrocity and would continue to live with every indignity and atrocity, turning away our eyes and keeping silent in the vain hope that we would remain untouched.

The boys spoke of taking up arms, of shooting NKVD agents, of having their revenge, but calmer heads always prevailed—and we girls were usually among them. Don't be idiotic, we would say. If you assassinate a Bolshevik, they'll arrest all of you and all of us and ship us out to Kazakhstan or, God forbid, Siberia. Eventually, as rumors of war with Germany intensified, the boys argued that, if the Germans attacked the Soviets, we could just watch these two Goliaths fight it out and then, once they were both exhausted, raise our flag above our land. Despite all this talk of war between Hitler and Stalin, few of us really believed it would take place. They were friends and allies. The newspapers slavishly praised the German Führer. Weren't the boys indulging in bravado and confusing their wishes for reality?

On June 22, 1941, those wishes became reality and the world I knew disintegrated once more. My life was stood on its head: the past vanished, as did the people I associated with it, the present asserted itself with an unimaginably ugly brutality, and, all at once, the future seemed as uncertain as the horizon was distant on a ship crossing the Atlantic. I had lost Mama and America. I had lost Mike and Stefan. I had lost Poland. And now I lost—what? I felt no loyalty to the oppressive entity the Russians called Soviet Ukraine, but for two years it was where my home had been located. That entity wasn't my home, but my home and my life were there and now that *there* had disappeared, just as Mike had, when his train pulled out of the station and the sun's reflection off the window obliterated his image. This time, even more so than in the past, the end of one life was implicated in the end of lives, with death, but with the kind of death I could never, in my worst nightmares, have envisioned.

The German army had not yet marched into Przemyślany when, on June 30 and July 1, the Bolsheviks packed their things and fled. At once, the streets were empty and the tattered posters of Stalin were the only reminders of two years of Soviet rule. Tato said we should stay at home and wait. For what, however, none of us knew and, I suspect, neither did he. Wait we did, but for only one hour, and then we crept out of the house like hungry mice and espied our neighbors standing about aimlessly in the street. The men smoked, the women held their children's hands, and no one spoke. I walked up Pocztowa and saw knots of agitated people, mostly Ukrainians, heading toward the right. I joined them. Some walked with impassive expressions on their faces, some held handkerchiefs to their eyes and had been crying. There was talk of the prison.

There was talk of gunshots and screams in the night that had come from within the prison. We reached linden alley and turned right.

The prison was in the basement of a neat red-brick building of three floors. I knew it well from my interviews with the NKVD. That it was perfectly quiet immediately struck me as odd: some twenty or thirty boys had been incarcerated in the last few weeks and one of them was Stefa's husband, Bohdan. Someone tried opening the door, but it was locked. Someone else knocked, while others went around toward the back. The rest of us stood nervously, shuffling our feet in the dust and feeling anxious at the awful stillness of the heavy air. Something was very wrong and all of us could feel it. The prisoners should have been shouting, they should have been crying out for help. Had they been evacuated with the fleeing Bolsheviks?

As the crowd pressed forward, we heard a shout from the back: "There are graves here! The ground has been freshly dug!" And then there erupted a cacophony of voices: "Where? Where?" "Here, in the back." "Shovels, bring shovels." "The women to the back, please. The men come forward. We need you to dig." "Graves, oh my God, graves!" I began praying and crying and hoping against hope that Bohdan wouldn't be in one of them. After a few minutes a terrible stench rose from the earth and enveloped us like the limpid air of a hot summer afternoon. The doors had been broken down and a few people ran inside. Their cries reverberated throughout the basement and resembled the howling of mad dogs. I shuddered and prayed still harder. And again the shrieks: "Blood! There is blood everywhere! Oh, my God, there is blood everywhere! What did they do, the Bolsheviks? What in God's name did they do to our boys?"

Then they pulled out the first body. And then they pulled out the second body and the third and the fourth and the fifth—and sixth and seventh and eighth and ninth and tenth and eleventh and twelfth and thirteenth and fourteenth and fifteenth and sixteenth and seventeenth and eighteenth and nineteenth and twentieth and twenty-first. None of them was our Bohdan. By now I had pushed my way into the backyard. The corpses lay on the green grass, like mangled fishes. They were covered with mud and blood and their clothes were torn and many were naked. Eyes and tongues were missing; tridents had been carved into chests; fingers, arms, and legs had been battered and broken; and, Heaven help us all, private parts had been ripped out, leaving gaping holes and bloody tissue between legs.

But none of them was Bohdan. Could he still be alive? I approached the largest pit, just to make sure, and, as I peered several meters into the abyss, I noticed what appeared to be an elbow in the mud. "There," I said quietly, knowing that the elbow was Bohdan's. "There is someone at the bottom." Two men climbed down, brushed away the mud from his shoulders, neck, and face, and lifted what remained of his long and broken body to the surface. His teeth had been knocked out, his eye sockets were empty, and his manhood was missing. He was naked and his hands were tied behind his back with barbed wire. He had been killed first and dumped into the pit first. Thank God, I thought, that Stefa is away. I looked at the heavens and asked God to punish the vile communists and their collaborators. I walked home with tears streaming down my face. When Tato saw me, he said only one word—"Bohdan?"—and I nodded. He embraced me and held me tightly and I thought of Mama, who lay in a pit in Fall River and could no longer comfort me.

There is too much death. Wherever I am, wherever I go, the scythe follows, oftentimes so closely that I can hear it slice the air and nip at my heels. It chased me from Fall River and it greeted me in Przemyślany. Father Kowcz says we should be thankful to God for the wonder of His creation. I am. And yet, part of me wants to know why there are so many endings amid so few beginnings. I understand: it is God's plan and I trust in God and His plan. Whatever happens is, I am certain, part of that plan. It may strike us as good or it may strike us as bad, but only God ultimately knows what is and what is not good or bad. Of these things I have absolutely no doubt: and yet and yet, I confess to wishing there was less death. Instead, wherever I look, wherever I go, I see doom or impending doom.

The dead continue to live in my thoughts and in my soul. Mama has never abandoned me, not even for a second since the day she left us. I carry her with me, in me, at all times. I speak to her, I pray with her, I ask her for advice, I ask her for comfort. And she always provides it, unfailingly. But the others, the dead and the soon-to-be-dead, are in my heart and in my soul as well. This is an exceedingly heavy burden for any person to carry. And I am tired, very, very tired. As the song goes: *"Kamień na kamieniu, na kamieniu kamień, a na tym kamieniu jeszcze jeden kamień." There's a stone on the stone, and on the stone there's a stone, and on that stone is yet another stone.* There are too many stones in life and sometimes I feel like Sisyphus.

When all the bodies were exhumed, arrayed, cleaned, and interred in a common grave in the cemetery, the mass grief could finally end and something like a normal existence—I purposely don't say life—could resume. But not until the parents or relatives came to the prison and identified the remains. Mrs. Trofimiak lost three sons and her anguished cries filled the yard like a siren, subsiding at times, only to resume with still greater force. Her wet face glowed, her swollen eyes were red, and her white lips quivered like the wings of a sparrow in flight. Her husband, no less pale and visibly fighting tears, held her by the waist as she pushed him away and attempted to throw herself on the rotting corpses of her sons. I knew the boys well, but never suspected they might have been political. Perhaps they had been arrested in some sweep? Perhaps, unlike Bohdan, they had no quarrels with the Russians? No, they, too, hated the Soviet Union. Every one of us did. They may not have been in the underground, but they were patriots and were deemed enemies of the people by the barbarians who laid waste to our land.

My father and I went to identify Bohdan. Although I thought I was fully prepared for what awaited us, I was still shocked by the pasty whiteness of his swollen flesh and the gaping brown gashes on his face, chest, and groin. Our handsome young Bohdan had been transformed into a monstrous thing. Tato visibly shuddered. When he was calm again, he turned to me. "Why did they mutilate him?" His voice trembled. "Was he already dead or was he still alive?" "He had to have been alive," I whispered. "The Bolsheviks torture the living and they desecrate the dead." "They are savages," he mumbled, while making the sign of the cross. "May the hand of the Lord strike them down." "Amen," I replied.

Stefa had been staying with Bohdan's family in Zbaraż and, when she finally completed her Odyssey and returned home, we escorted her to the cemetery. She promptly fainted upon seeing the burial mound. After she revived, she began crying hysterically and Tato and I, like poor Mrs. Trofimiak's little husband, had to keep her from throwing herself on the grave in grief. As we dragged her away, I began reciting the Our Father and kissing her crimson cheeks. Suddenly, her body went limp again and she almost fell to the ground, murmuring, "Bohdan, my Bohdan." Once home, Tato and I gave Stefa tea with rum and placed her in bed.

It was soon after the bodies were discovered that little Ivanko was beaten to a pulp and thrown into one of the blood-smeared prison cells. No one felt sorry for him. I know I didn't; neither did Stefa. The Ukrainians who had lost friends or relatives in the prison patrolled the streets and hunted down the collaborators who had sustained the communist terror for two years. Several were caught, but none was despised as much as Ivanko. Knowing what awaited them if they stayed, most of the criminals had fled with the retreating Bolsheviks. The mood was ugly and vengeance was in the air. Przemyślany seethed with contradictory passions and the somnolent town I knew so well had ceased to exist.

Stefa remained despondent for days. She had no appetite and sat in the garden, silently and motionlessly. Tato devoted himself to his wheat field and cast sad glances at her. I stayed with Stefa for hours every day, but there was nothing to say and nothing to do, but wait and hope and pray. For what? We really did not know. Father Kowcz would come by, usually in the early evening after his day's work was completed, and try to provide her with solace, invoking God's will and reminding her of Bohdan's ascension to Heaven. I would serve tea and cake. Tato and my stepmother would usually join us, but Stefa's mood rarely improved.

I began having terrible nightmares. It was always the same image: the elbow at the bottom of the black pit, Bohdan's broken, beaten, tortured body, and the brilliantly red blood that seeped into the grass and spattered the prison floor and walls. Bohdan never moved and never spoke in my dreams. He just lay there. I wanted to look into his eyes, but there were none, and I wanted to take his hands, but they were tied behind his back with wire. The nightmares would awaken me and I would sit upright, panic-stricken, and breathe deeply in the dark and, as much as I tried to banish the image of the bloody corpse, the slimy entrails, and the gaping holes, I could not. Once my beating heart resumed its regular rhythm, I would lower my body onto the bed and, at the very moment my back touched the mattress and my eyes closed, it seemed to me that I, too, was a corpse, a bloody, mangled, tortured piece of rotting human flesh. And how could my dear Mama not come to mind then? At least she reposed peacefully in her grave. Had she also suffered before she died? Had she cried, asked God to help her, and implored Tato to do something, anything, to keep her alive, so that she could take care of her children? I didn't know and I never would know and all I could know was that Mama was gone and Mykhasko was gone and now Bohdan was gone. There is too much death, much too much death, in my life and in my memories and in the very air I breathe.

When the Germans roared into town, the townsfolk greeted them with bread and salt and songs and smiles. And hope. They were our liberators and they were going to free us from the Bolshevik yoke. They were going to give us independence, freedom, and dignity. How straight they marched. How clean they looked. How shiny were their helmets, rifles, and boots. The dust didn't settle on their uniforms and the glare of the sun never made them wince. The cultured Germans had driven out the brutish Russians. We were ecstatic. So were our Polish relatives. Even our Jewish neighbors had high hopes that the "New Order" might be an improvement on the Soviet paradise. Moszko the barber told Tato he was glad he hadn't fled with the Bolsheviks. The nation of Goethe, Beethoven, and Heine would treat Jews well and all the rumors he had heard had to have been exaggerations or lies. All would be well, he said. Didn't Tato agree? Tato said something about war being a terrible thing and that we, and Jews in particular, should be careful, but Moszko shook his head and smiled and said that all would definitely be well. He could feel it in the tips of his fingers and a barber's fingertips never lied. A portrait of Hitler now adorned his window.

Fanka had returned home on June 23 and I met my dearest friend a few times in the week before we unearthed the corpses. She was visibly on edge, saying she didn't know what to expect, but remained hopeful and placed her faith in the Lord. The three years she spent in Lviv had matured her: she was more elegant, more self-confident, more refined. And yet, beneath the fine exterior, she was still the same sweet companion who had strolled through town with Mańka and me so many times. I held her tightly in my arms and we cried, perhaps because both of us realized how much we had aged. "How you've changed!" she said to me. "What a beautiful woman you've become!" I responded. We spoke as if we hadn't seen each other in years, as if she hadn't visited her parents regularly and I, too, had not been to Lviv. But, this time, everything felt profoundly different. She had been forced to return by the outbreak of the war and I had been forced to stay by the fall of Poland. We were together again as a result of enormous forces that shaped the world and our little lives. We were the playthings of fate and we knew full well that, just as fate had brought us together again, so, too, it could tear us apart at a moment's notice, on an impetuous whim.

After Bohdan was killed, Fanka visited every day. We took long walks in the golden fields and cool forests, usually saying nothing, occasionally humming or singing our favorite songs from our days in the school choir, gathering wild poppies. How fragile and how delicate they were and how beautiful as well! They turned entire fields a bold and flaming red, but could barely survive for more than a day in a vase. Fanka placed them in my hair and, like nymphs, we ran through the woods holding hands. And, often, we just wept—without prompting, without purpose. There was a premonition, a foreboding in the air. Our lives would never be the same. The past had been brutally destroyed. The present hung somewhere between a murdered past and a hazy future. There was nothing for us to do but to trust in God and His providence.

Immediately after they stormed into town, the Germans locked several Jews inside the synagogue and set fire to it. Some townsfolk watched, shocked; others applauded, saying it was high time they paid for Bolshevik crimes. Aghast, Father Kowcz ran out of the church as soon as he heard the screaming and saw the black plumes rise into the sky and ordered the Germans to open the doors. Fortunately, most of the Jews survived, even though the impressively large synagogue burned to the ground. Next day, I saw Moszko approach my father with a worried expression on his face. Tato tried to reassure him, saying that such savagery couldn't possibly have been official policy, that this outburst had to have been spontaneous and exceptional. "Do you believe that, Tato?" I said. He shook his head in dismay and said: "The world has gone mad and I don't know what to believe."

Despite our growing unease, life went on. A Ukrainian lawyer who knew our family became the town mayor: he asked me to serve as his secretary and, desperate for work, I agreed. One of the first cases before the city court concerned little Ivanko: he was found guilty and condemned to a firing squad, but his sentence was commuted to life imprisonment after his father fell to his knees and begged for clemency. I felt both sorrow and embarrassment for the poor old man, who humiliated himself publicly for the sake of his criminal son. After the proceedings, Ivanko was led back to the prison where his victims had been tortured and killed. Crowds jeered and women spat at him and threw eggs. He walked with his head bowed and his hands tied behind his back, stumbling several times and almost falling, and each time his father caught him, eliciting catcalls. Reluctantly, I had to think of Christ.

A few years later, in what has to be one of the oddest twists of fate, Ivanko joined the Galizien Division: the Germans were taking everybody, even inmates. They gave him a gun, a helmet, and a uniform and he marched off to fight the same Bolsheviks who had once given him a gun to terrorize his own people. I didn't see Ivanko for some ten years, until, one day, when I was already in New York, we ran into each other on Second Avenue. He was now a high-ranking activist in some émigré organization. Little Ivan, the Bolshevik collaborator, had become an anti-Soviet nationalist and joined the ranks of the very people he had once denounced! He was trembling as he extended his hand. I refused to take it while telling him his secret was safe with me. I don't think he believed me and I never saw him again in New York.

Stefa grew larger with every day. While the family was joyfully awaiting the birth of her child, she remained as withdrawn and morose as ever. She ate and drank little and mostly sat on a garden bench Mike had cobbled together some years ago. Two or three times, she had strange accidents, tumbling down the stairs or tripping over a rug or a root. She never cried, she never looked alarmed, she never placed her hands soothingly on her belly. I began to suspect she was purposely trying to harm herself or, God forbid, the child. When I confronted her, she smiled sweetly and said of course not. I wasn't sure whether to believe her, so I kept my eye on her at all times. She regarded me with undisguised bitterness and I guessed I had been correct in my suspicions.

Bohdan's bloodied corpse continued to haunt me at night, but the horror of the occupation and the hardships of daily existence began to intrude on and squeeze out my memories and my nightmares. One day, the Germans ordered all Jews to wear yellow

Stars of David. Incredulous, we watched our neighbors comply, willingly and almost with relief, as if they had expected much worse and were happy this was all they had to do. Except for those who worked for the Judenrat or auxiliary police, most of Przemyślany's Jews took to appearing ever less frequently on the streets. When we encountered them outside, they averted their eyes and lowered their heads and hastened their step. Their houses turned silent

Kuba, the skinny Jewish boy who served as my assistant, continued to come to work until sometime in 1942, when he disappeared. We assumed he had met a tragic end, but, as he told me many years later, he had expected the worst and decided to flee. His German was almost flawless, so he was able to pass himself off as a Volksdeutscher and find a job as custodian of a game preserve in the Carpathians, where he regularly accompanied a high-ranking Gestapo office on boar hunts. When the Red Army approached in 1944, he joined the Polish communists and, after the war was over, studied law and became an assistant procurator in Silesia. He married a blue-blooded Polish woman, the daughter of a pre-war diplomat, and then, in 1965, while on a trip to Scandinavia, defected and settled in West Germany, where a local Jewish organization declined to give him assistance on the grounds that he was really Polish. What a simultaneously tragic and fortunate and ironic fate, I thought, when he told me of his adventures. Kuba gave me a photograph of himself just before he vanished: I should have guessed it was his parting gift.

Later that summer, it was our turn to experience the Nazi storm. As I was going to work one morning, I came upon several SS men pointing their guns at the heads of five of our boys who stood spread-eagled against the *cukernia*. German units had also positioned themselves in front of the post office, the mayor's office, and other official buildings and were leading groups of Ukrainians toward the prison. This was it, I thought: the crackdown had come and the shooting and killing would begin. That evening I ran into Vlodko and he told me our honeymoon with the Germans was over. Whatever illusions we had about their tolerating some form of

Ukrainian independence were, as he put it, "*kaputt*." It was time, once again, for the underground, for arms, and for resistance.

As I listened, my breathing suddenly felt constricted. Resistance could mean only one thing: more fighting, more bloodshed, more dying. I saw Bohdan lying at the bottom of the pit. Was that mixture of blood, mud, entrails, and excrement all the future held in store for us? Would the dying never end? And so we joined our Jewish and Polish neighbors in walking quickly, avoiding the Germans, and keeping our heads lowered. Home became the only refuge, the only place where we could breathe normally, without fear of being spied on, denounced, or arrested. There was talk of German camps. There was talk of mass shootings of Jews. Fanka became as worried as everybody else. She wore her star and laughed about it, saying a star had also heralded Christ's birth, but it was clear, at least to me, that her laughter wasn't genuine: the sparkle in her eyes was gone.

In early 1942 Stefa gave birth to a boy she named Bohdan. She was thin and frail and hadn't been taking care of herself for months: labor lasted close to twenty hours and she screamed and moaned for most of the time. Every once in a while, Sara, the midwife, emerged from the room and asked for a glass of water or sat down and closed her eyes for a minute or two. But we could tell from the expression on her face that the delivery was going well. And then we heard a baby's cry and we knew the ordeal was over. Sara called me and Tato and my stepmother inside. Stefa looked as broken as a corpse, but she was holding the child in her arms and, when she raised her eyes ever so slightly, we saw they were glowing.

Little Bohdan brought new life into our gloomy house. All of us helped with the chores, not because they were onerous, but because they kept us from contemplating the horrible things taking place outside. German, Jewish, and Ukrainian policemen had herded the Jews through a barbed-wire gate into a ghetto located just across Pocztowa. The empty Jewish houses on our street turned into soundless tombs. They exuded so many tears and so much heartrending suffering that I purposely avoided walking in the dreadful no-man's land between them and the barbed-wire fence. On one side were the former lives of our neighbors. Somewhere on the other side were those very same neighbors, but without their former lives. Their confinement served as a constant reminder to those of us who remained outside in what passed for freedom of the unspeakable brutality that human beings who violate God's commandments are capable of committing.

The ghetto guards followed a route that took them past our house every few minutes. After nightfall, when we were sure nobody was looking, our aged father would run across the street, toss a potato or onion over the barbed wire, and quickly retreat. Did any of the inmates find the food or was it confiscated by the Jewish police? We never found out. Tato insisted it did not matter. Father Kowcz also said God commanded us to help our neighbors: he baptized hundreds of Jews who believed that, as Christians, they might be saved. They were wrong and the good Father was arrested for his charitable work and taken to some camp and incinerated.

Little Bohdan kept us busy, reminding us that life always followed on the heels of death and that death was now all around us. There had never been any escape from it, as I had learned as a little girl. But the all-pervasive sight and smell of death was something entirely new: none of us knew how to cope. At least the nationalists could plan their revenge, collect weapons, and prepare to go underground. But we civilians were fated—or doomed—to stay above ground, where there was no respite from the blackness that had descended on and swallowed our lives. The Poles and the Jews were just as despondent and just as impotent. There was nothing to be done. Resistance seemed impossible. Everybody accepted the horrible reality and marched toward Armageddon. The entire town had become worse than a ghetto. It had become a graveyard.

What is there to say about the remainder of my time in Przemyślany? The Jews were massacred, although Fanka survived thanks to Vlodko, who hid her and her parents in a tiny space behind the pantry in some peasant's house. Her mother couldn't stand the confinement, went mad, and died. Fanka then found refuge in a Greek Catholic monastery. Her father and brother were shot. Another brother joined the Bolsheviks. Vlodko blew his brains out after he and several other guerrillas were surrounded by Russian troops. Fanka became a nun and lived in Przemyślany in a house occupied by several other nuns. We corresponded regularly since the sixties and she died with God's name on her lips at the age of ninety-three.

Eventually, the Germans began killing the Jews and the Ukrainians began fighting the Germans. Meanwhile, the Russians were advancing and everyone knew what that meant. Expecting an imminent German withdrawal, Ukrainian and Polish guerrillas tried to establish control of the territory before the communists arrived: armed skirmishes, clandestine killings, and the burning of houses and property became daily occurrences. I could never have imagined such savagery. What little remained of the town was dying before our eyes and, in mid-1944, Stefa, little Bohdan, my half-brother Slavko, and I joined some friends who were fleeing west. I held my father in my arms for several minutes and couldn't believe we were parting forever. His thick white mustache tickled my cheeks as he kissed me repeatedly and assured me they would be fine, that the family was strong, that I should take care of Mykhasko when I reached America. I climbed aboard the truck with one little suitcase and waved until he disappeared. I wanted to cry, but the sound of exploding shells in the east forced me to gather my wits and realize that this death—of my town, of my father, of my family—also promised me something approximating life.

We bounced along for a week before reaching Slovakia. Little Bohdan, who was just two and a half years old, was terrified throughout the journey, sitting in Stefa's lap or mine and whimpering incessantly. The roads were clogged with refugees just like us and we drove slowly, continually swerving to the left or to the right so as to avoid knots of haggard-looking people carrying little bundles or dusty suitcases. Crossing the Carpathians was especially dangerous: the forests were full of Polish and Soviet partisans who, it was rumored, were hunting down Ukrainians and skinning them alive. Slovakia, with its neat villages and ubiquitous church domes, looked like paradise to us and we settled near Prešov. Stefa was hired as a maid by some rich peasant in Krompachy; I joined the household of one Father Krlička in Helcmanovce. The Slovak priest and his wife worked me to the bone and, one day, when she and their five children were away, he exposed himself while I was doing the dishes in the kitchen. It was time to go. Fortunately, Mike was discharged from the military and, when he returned to New York in early 1946, I began laying concrete plans for my return to the land of my birth.

In all that time in Slovakia, I had no word from my family. Where was Fanka? Where was Maňka? Where was Stefan? Were they alive? Were they dead? I had no way of knowing. The war had destroyed everything. It had destroyed our town and its inhabitants. It had destroyed my family and friends. And it had also destroyed my memories. What was there to remember? There had been good times and good memories, but the bad times and bad memories so outweighed them that it became far easier to forget and refuse to remember than to remember. But a person without memories is not a human being. Those two and a half years in Slovakia transformed me into a beast of burden, and not just because of the terrible work load I had. It was far worse. I was cut off from my past. I was cut off from the future. And I was even cut off from the present. When you have no one to talk to, when you have no one to listen to your stories, when you have no one to remember the past with you, you are dead. And in Slovakia I had died. Mike raised me from the dead by paying for my passage across the Atlantic.

Our journey began at the American embassy in Prague. All I had was my passport and the little suitcase I took with me when leaving home. After two years with the priest and his family, my possessions were even sparser than before: two dresses, one nightshirt, a blouse, a skirt, one pair of underwear, two pairs of socks, a sweater, one pair of shoes, a hat, and a coat. Along with some mementoes from home: photographs, a prayer book, a crucifix, several holy pictures, and an embroidered pillow cover sewn by my mother. I had come to Slovakia looking like a bedraggled refugee and I was leaving Czechoslovakia looking like a bedraggled refugee. Nothing changes; life is a silent river.

The bus took us up the length of Germany. I was shocked to see how devastated the land was. Few buildings were intact and the surviving structures resembled a craggy mountain landscape. The roads had huge holes that made for excruciatingly slow travel. But it was the people who shocked me most. The Germans I saw through the window were almost all women bundled up in thick coats, with scarves wrapped around their heads and heavy shoes on their formerly dainty feet. They looked like backward peasants from high up in the Carpathians. The few men I saw were all as thin as boys. Their clothes, several sizes too large, hung from their bony bodies like the sheets one drapes over furniture to safeguard it from dust. But these men actually appeared to be covered with dust. I couldn't see their faces from the bus, but I was sure their downwardly sloped heads concealed dead eyes. These men had seen too much and they had done too much. I thought of my town and the catastrophe that befell it. Perhaps the Germans who looked like tramps had once been the proud soldiers and SS men who had come to usher in the New Order that ended in devastation for everybody. Here, too, there was death and more death. In Germany, even the living were dead.

From Copenhagen we took a ferry to Stockholm. In both cities the Americans put us up in hotels and provided us with food. My rooms were tiny, but each night I slept soundly and without any nightmarish apparitions. And, besides potatoes and some canned vegetables, they actually served meat: small pieces that were tough to chew, but meat nonetheless. But I couldn't eat it. My family might be starving. Fanka was certainly hungry. Stefan could never fend for himself. And my friends were dying in bunkers. How could I eat like a queen? I wrapped the meat in a napkin and took it with me. There might be need of it on the boat. One never knew.

And so I embarked on my second transatlantic voyage. The Gripsholm was a majestic ship that shone in the sun and seemed large enough to accommodate all of Przemyślany. They checked our documents, assigned us to our rooms, and explained the safety procedures. How could my thoughts not rush back to the spring of 1923, twenty-four long years ago, when Tato and I had led Stefa and Mike on board and coddled and reassured them during the vicious storms and high waves? I was ten years old then. I was thirty-four now. Lifetimes had passed in the interim. Worlds had collided, universes had exploded, and an infinity of time had passed through my fingers like sand through a sieve. The children I had known in Fall River were all as old as I was and, if I saw them, I was sure we wouldn't recognize one another. The friends, relatives, and acquaintances I had in Przemyślany were dead, had fled, or been deported to Siberia. I had left a world that disappeared for a world that had also disappeared. And now I was leaving that non-existent world for a country that existed only in my imagination and only in association with Mike. I could see the tall buildings of New York, the mountains and forests of Oregon, and the palm trees of California. Where, exactly, among these skyscrapers, mountains, and trees would I fit in and find a home? I had no idea, except that Mike would be my home. But would Mykhasko recognize me, his big sister? Would I recognize him? After all, nine years had passed since he left as a boy. Now he was a man. I had been a young woman then. Now I, too, was approaching maturity. Would he still be my little brother?

These sobering thoughts quickly dissipated as soon as we got out to sea and the high waves and incessant rocking of this majestic ship-turned-rowboat confined me to my bunk for the duration of the voyage. I ate nothing and drank only tea. I recall being taken outside for some fresh air, but otherwise spent the two weeks in my night dress and in a state of near-delirium. All thoughts of Mike, America, and the skyscrapers of New York vanished and, instead, all I could think of and see, with a clarity that terrified me and compounded my misery, was the killings, shootings, and explosions, the rumbling of tanks, the screeching of diving planes, and the wailing of sirens that had accompanied my life for three years. Fanka, Vlodko, Jenta, Stefan, Mańka, Moszko, and too many other ghostly apparitions flitted before my eyes and disappeared, only to return, reminding me that they were dead or dying and that I should have stayed and shared their sad fate with them.

The bomb that almost killed us kept dropping from the sky. I heard the enormity of the explosion and felt the terror we all shared as the smoke lifted, the dust settled, and our family realized we were still alive and the house was, miraculously, still standing. I saw Bohdan's muddy body at the bottom of the pit, his arms and legs and head at odd angles to his torso, almost as if he were a crushed porcelain doll. And I saw his bloody corpse as it lay beside the other bloody corpses on the grass that was trampled and muddy and red and the horror of that grass was almost as horrible as the horror of the corpses.

And throughout all these terrifying visions the emotion I felt most powerfully was helplessness. I was powerless to halt the visions and prevent the brutalities of our occupiers and their destruction of our town, our people, and our neighbors. Such all-encompassing impotence is, I suspect, the worst feeling in the world: to be unable to do anything about the crushing circumstances that are depriving you of your ability to breathe. I understood then, in my bunk, the incomprehensible passivity of our Jewish neighbors. They entered the ghettos without resisting; they walked to the forests where they were killed without fighting or fleeing. It was almost as if they willingly bowed to the authority of the Germans and their own council and police. But just how were they to resist? How were we? How was anyone? When you are bound to your bed or to your fate, what is there to do but succumb to God's will and accept what He has in store for you?

At times my bunk felt like a coffin: I was buried alive, barely able to inhale, wanting to flail my arms and legs, but unable to move them, even a centimeter, and feeling that I was slowly joining the corpses arrayed in the trampled, muddy, scarlet grass in the prison yard. Did I shout? I think I did and, when I did, a voice would soothe me and a wet cloth caressed my brow and cheeks. But the wetness of the cloth reminded me of fresh blood and only heightened my fear. The pressure and the presence of death subsided only when I slept and failed to dream. That may have been for hours or for minutes. I remember only the wave of exhaustion and relief that overcame me whenever I opened my eyes and, if only for a brief moment, felt as if the grave had not yet been fully filled and labored breathing could resume.

Where were Fanka and Mańka and Vlodko and Stefan and Stefa and Tato and Bohdan and Mike? Why didn't they save me from the grip of decay? Why didn't they extend their strong hands and pull me out of this abyss? Didn't they see the bloody, mangled, muddy bodies all round me? Didn't they realize I could neither inhale nor exhale with so much dead flesh and so much dead life and so many dead hopes, fears, expectations, and loves surrounding me? The abandonment I felt was total and the despair was equally great. Life was over. I was dead; everything was dead. The death that had followed me throughout my entire life had finally claimed me as its victim.

And then, one morning, there came my resurrection. The ship had stopped rocking. The foghorn blew incessantly and the commotion of people scurrying about and talking awoke me. The tombstone had been uncovered and, when I opened my weary eyes, I sensed my ordeal was over. The journey had come to an end. We were in New York harbor. I raised myself on my right elbow and surveyed the other women. One of them smiled and asked if I wanted some tea. I nodded and dropped my numb legs over the side of the bunk. She handed me a cup and a piece of toast. Nothing in my life—not even Mama's pastries—had ever been quite as delicious and I savored every sip and rolled the chunks of bread among my teeth and caressed them with my tongue. "When will we be disembarking?" I asked weakly. One more night on board, someone said, and we'll be in New York in the morning. That night I slept as I used to sleep in Fall River. And in the morning there was Mike. He had grown leaner and more muscular and his hair was no longer neatly parted in the middle. I recognized him immediately, but he must have been shocked to see an emaciated brunette with a ratty coat approach and embrace and kiss him. "My little brother," I said through my tears. "Welcome to America, Manya," he replied. "Come, let's go home. You must be hungry."

How loud and dirty this terrifying city was! Cars, wagons, horses, trams, and people, people, people—all running, all hurrying, all walking with their heads bent and their hands clutching lumpy bags or leather cases or hats or scarves, as if they were fleeing the Gestapo or NKVD. Below you were concrete and asphalt. To the sides were bricks and concrete. And above were bricks and concrete and tiny slivers of unwelcoming, metallic sky. I held Mike's arm tightly as he led the way among the throngs. He strode confidently. He knew exactly where he was going and I could see that this madhouse was home for my little brother. It was I who was his helpless little sister.

We finally arrived at his building on East Tenth Street. Fall River hadn't been anything like this. Trash lined the gutters and dirty children were playing in the street. We climbed the squeaky, dark staircase to the third or fourth floor and walked along a brown corridor smelling of grease, cabbage, and garlic. Mike inserted a flat key into a lock, turned it twice, and pushed open a creaky door. He pulled on a string and a lone yellow light bulb hanging from a twisted wire caught fire. We stood in a small kitchen, with a table, two chairs, an iron stove, an ice box, and, of all things, a bath tub. Two tiny rooms followed, with one—"This'll be yours," Mike said—looking out onto the street below. I removed my coat and held him tightly. He heard me suppress my sobs and said, "It'll be fine, Manya. You'll see, it'll be fine." He led me to a small sofa. "Sit down. I'll make a sandwich. Would you like one? And some tea. Or would you like something stronger? And then you'll tell me everything about Tato and Stefa and the others." As he went into the kitchen, I thought: Oh, Mykhasko, don't you know? All the others are gone! There is no one left. It's just you and me, little brother.

We lived off Mike's savings at first, but I soon found work cleaning apartments and washing dishes in little neighborhood cafeterias and our lives improved. I was able to buy myself a dress, blouses, shoes, and, eventually, a coat. Later that year, Stefa and little Bohdan arrived and Mike and I met them at the same pier where I had disembarked feeling dead to the world just a short while ago. And now, here I was, shivering on the windswept pier with my brother, waiting for the ship to dock, the gangway to be lowered, and my sister and nephew to appear. She hadn't changed, but the boy had grown and, if she hadn't been leading him by the hand, I might not have recognized him.

Stefa joined me in the front room, while Mike and little Bohdan took the middle room. Stefa took to cleaning houses in the Bronx and, with three modest incomes, we managed quite well, perhaps not by American standards, but certainly by those of back home. She brought news of the family. Slavko had entered a monastery in Slovakia and was considering the priesthood: a few years later, the communists would imprison him for his vocation. Tato didn't write—no one in western Ukraine was writing or receiving letters—but Stefa had heard from some traveler that, even though Przemyślany was under siege by the secret police, our immediate family had managed to remain intact.

That Christmas, for the first time in almost ten years, we sang carols and decorated a small tree. Mike had left in 1938 and we were certain we'd never see him again. The war had come and he feared we wouldn't survive. Instead, here we were, all together at last, in a tiny apartment in Manhattan celebrating Christ's birth and our reunion in America. We remembered our mother who lay in Fall

River and we cried at the thought that we would never be reunited with our father. But the three of us—the three natives of both Fall River and Przemyślany—were together again and that was a miracle for which we were immensely grateful.

Mike had changed: he was thinner and stronger and looked more experienced and mature and, when he smiled, his smile concealed more than it revealed. He no longer confided in me as he had before. He'd withdraw into his own thoughts and remain silent for hours on end, chain-smoking during those absences, as if he were concentrating on something important that was eluding him. Sometimes he hummed some melody, listened to the radio, or rambled on about people or places that meant nothing to me. When I asked him to explain, he'd grow irritable, rub out his cigarette in the ash tray, and leave the room. One night, I heard him moaning in his sleep and repeating a name that sounded like Wanda. A Polish girl named Wanda had lived in Przemyślany, but she was much older than Mike and I couldn't imagine he meant her. When I asked him next day who Wanda was, he glared at me for a few seconds, dropped his tea cup into the sink, and stormed out of the kitchen. Mike also complained of pains in his abdomen. He had no appetite, he said, because his digestive system wasn't well. It was the army's fault and they should pay him for it, but refused. Dark forces were conspiring against him. Among them was the Queen of England. Needless to say, his ravings worried us.

Fortunately, Mike had his camera. He carried it about wherever he went, clicking at strangers, lampposts, hydrants, cars, buildings, and empty spaces, sometimes with film, mostly without. "It's too expensive," he said, "and I don't need it anyway." When he held the camera in his hands, he was the same Mykhasko I had known and loved for so many years. His irascibility disappeared, his impatience vanished. He appeared happy, adjusting the focus, looking through the lens, stepping back, stepping forward, and constantly mumbling under his breath. Whom or what was he photographing I didn't know. Nor did I care.

Mike loved the boy and little Bohdan loved him. They'd roam the streets for hours and, when they returned home after one of their outings, Bohdan always had a grin on his face and Mike always held his hand tightly. When the boy began attending kindergarten, it was Mike who insisted on dropping off and picking up little Bohdan. He missed the boy and, perhaps as a result, his obsession with the camera grew. When Stefa and Bohdan moved into an even tinier apartment of their own in the same building, all of us cried, although just why I honestly don't know. Except for Mike, who chain-smoked silently and, after carrying Stefa's last piece of luggage upstairs, walked out of her apartment without saying a word, not even good-night.

Where were Mike's thoughts during all these extended silences? What was he photographing so frenetically? I never knew. But I distinctly felt that, once again, my little brother was leaving, perhaps had already left, me. He was on a train or a ship or in some camp in the mountains or in some barracks in California. And only once in a while would he come home and smile at me with the same warmth I remembered so fondly. But life went on, as it always does, and soon Oleksa arrived and we got married and then we had a child. Only Mike's life appeared mired in one place. He still had no job, he still sat silently for hours with his cigarettes and radio, he still wandered the streets with his camera, and he still spoke of people and places that had no meaning for me. And, when he slept, Wanda's name continued to escape his feverish lips.

In the meantime, death continued to haunt me. I received a letter from home, from a cousin, informing me that Stefan had died in 1945. Three years had gone by and I had had no inkling. He had a child and, after she died before reaching her first birthday, he died— of tuberculosis, of grief, of despair. And his final words, on his deathbed, had been: "Manya, Manya." Was that true? I didn't know and I could never know, but my heart broke again. How many times can a heart shatter like a mirror? And then Tato died and Oleksa's mother died and his younger brother was arrested and deported to Siberia, where he eventually vanished, and, just as life seemed to be returning to normal, just as we were adjusting to New York and America, the past seized us by our necks and reminded us that there was no such thing as a new beginning, that one was always hostage to history, that death never went away. I should have known it never would, but a new country and marriage and a child seemed to suggest it just might. That was an illusion, of course, like every human joy, I suppose.

And then we lost Mike. He stopped going out altogether. He sat in his room with the door closed, smoking and pointing the camera at empty walls and making odd clucking sounds. His nightmares became worse and his mumblings about Wanda never left his lips. One day, a neighbor followed Mike up the staircase to the roof. Mike was standing at the edge, his arms raised up against the sky, and looking down at the street. The neighbor asked what he was up to and Mike said Wanda had told him to go there and look closely at the asphalt below. Another time, I came home and found Mike sitting at the table in the dark, deliberately pulling the kitchen knife across his forearm. The blood didn't trouble him and he seemed completely indifferent to the pain. "What in God's name are you doing?" I shouted. He raised his head calmly and answered: "Removing the poison from my veins. They're trying to kill me." "Who, Mykhasko, who?" I sobbed. "Edna and the Queen of England," he replied and continued with his cutting motion. I grabbed the knife and, instead of reacting angrily, he reached for a cigarette, lit it, and stuck it between his teeth. "Don't worry," he said as the cigarette bobbed in his mouth, "Edna's out to get me, but I won't let her." Edna? I wanted to ask. Who is this Edna? But all I could see was the blood-spattered table and floor and all I could think of was the prison in Przemyślany and Bohdan's corpse at the bottom of the pit.

Stefa and I conferred. We had no choice and we knew it. Our little brother was ill and had to be placed in some institution. Oleksa and Mike's veteran friends took him to a hospital not far from where we lived. I couldn't go: I hadn't the strength to see my little brother interred in a tomb where I feared he would remain forever. Another death descended on our lives, another death clouded our present and future, another death reminded us we were pawns of fate. But, worst of all, this time the blood was, even if metaphorically, on our hands. We had, once again, to bow to God's oftentimes incomprehensibly cruel will.

CLINICAL SUMMARY

Date of admission: March 27, 1951

Date of summary: July 10, 1951

Family History: Father's name, John B., born in Poland; occupation shoemaker, was successful. Mother's maiden name: Anna D., born in Poland. No member of the family has shown peculiar conduct or mental disease. None has been alcoholic, no one has shown any anti-social conduct, such as conflicts with the law, arrests, bad habits, etc.

Personal History: Patient was born July 3, 1919 in Fall River, Mass. He didn't have an instrumental birth. At the age of 4 he went to Europe with his father and two sisters. It was after their mother's death. In Poland he lived in a small town, Przemyślany, there he attended the public school. Patient left school at the age of 14 after he reached the 7th grade. He then worked in a grocery store as a salesman until 1938. At this time he came to the United States. Patient was not married. When patient was in Poland he was healthy, happy, strong, had many friends who liked him very much because he was sociable. He belonged to a sport club and very often used to play football. He had a very good voice and used to sing in the school or church choir. He left Europe at the age of 19 years old and came to New York. Patient's two sisters came to the U.S. in 1947. They lived with him. At this time, patient was very unhappy, sat in a chair for hours staring in one place. He was nervous, would argue at any little thing. He often said that people didn't like him, were jealous, did not let him go to work. He was supported by his two sisters.

Onset of Psychosis: When patient's two sisters came to the United States in 1947, they noticed a change in him. Each year had shown more symptoms. In 1949 and 1950 he did not want to go anyplace, slept and sat at home in his little room, talked to himself and played the radio day and night. He avoided people, closed all doors and windows, did not want to eat. He said that some person by the name of Wanda came to his house and gave him all sorts of trouble. He broke all glass doors in his apartment, injured himself in the legs, fingers, face with a knife, said Wanda told him to do this. In 1951 patient became worse. He wanted to jump from the roof, wanted to die because this girl Wanda told him to do it. The people in the apartment building started to become afraid and called the police. He was then sent to the hospital.

Bellevue Hospital: Admitted March 15, 1951. Physical condition: Physically negative. Mental condition: This patient believes that when he goes to bed at night women bind him up and then torture him. He believes that Bing Crosby has been drugging him the past two years. Patient is disorganized, disconnected and affect is quite inappropriate. Delusions are bizarre. Insight and judgment is nil.

State Hospital: A 32-year old ex-service man who was brought to Bellevue by friends because of his obvious psychotic behavior. His condition is characterized by bizarre delusions of poisoning and of being doped. He hallucinates, attributes remarks and programs he hears on the radio to himself and uses them as proof of his condition. He is somewhat effeminate in his mannerisms and describes himself as being very, very nice most of the time "as I am now," but then there are periods when the dope gets to a certain part of his brain and he draws a blank and does not know what he does. Orientation intact, insight lacking, judgment defective. Impression: Dementia Praecox: Paranoid.

Initial Presentation: April 10, 1951: Diagnosis: Dementia Praecox: Hebephrenic.

Subsequent Course: On admission patient appeared rather simple and shallow. At times he becomes tense, agitated, and disturbed. His speech was frequently circumstantial and he exhibited occasional inappropriate smiling, and revealed a wealth of delusional material of a paranoid nature. Patient did not participate in the ward routine and did not mix with other patients. On May 31 he was transferred to the Veterans Division. At this time he was quite delusional and appeared depressed. At present patient admits hearing voices. He is flat, dull and apathetic. Impression is poor. He is oriented and shows no marked memory impairment. Physical condition is satisfactory.

Diagnosis: Dementia Praecox: Hebephrenic.

Condition: Unimproved.

Incompetent.

We visited Mike several times a year and, after Stefa got married and her husband bought a car, we could drive out to Long Island with potato dumplings, stuffed cabbage rolls, and pastries. Mike was usually glad to see us, but his attention span was short and, after a half hour or so, he'd usually get impatient and start chain-smoking. It was clear that he wanted us to leave and we would, feeling both sadness and relief. Our husbands cracked jokes, while Stefa and I told him about our lives and especially about our children. He always asked about little Bohdan and, as my children got older, about them as well. Why didn't they visit? He'd ask. They're so busy, we'd say, but how could I tell my brother that my children had no idea they had an uncle an hour away on Long Island? I could no more tell him than I could tell them. Was it shame? Fear? Force of habit? Guilt? All I know is that Stefa and I could never forget that we, his loving sisters, had removed our little brother, our shy Mykhasko, from the land of the living. We loved him and we had done our duty: we saved him from himself and his demons, but we also lost him. Consolation was impossible: who was to console us and how were we to be consoled? He had lost his soul. And we had lost part of ours as well.

Chapter 3
Stefa

Stefa, the youngest sibling, was born in 1921, two years after Mike and seven after Manya. Their mother died one year later, in 1922, and then, in 1923, the family returned to Przemyślany. More accurately, it was their father, Jan-Ivan, who returned, while his children only accompanied him. Naturally, Stefa had no recollection of Fall River. Manya told her fabulous stories of Division Street and South Park and the enormous house they lived in and Mama's wonderful cooking and Mike had some memories of playing ball with the boys in the street and eating snails, but Stefa could only listen and smile and shake her head in disbelief. America could just as easily have been Africa or Asia. Fall River, the Portuguese, and Narragansett Bay were unpronounceable words, while textile mills, smokestacks, and trolley cars that went bing-bing-bing were unimaginable objects that belonged in fairy tales.

Mama was Tato's new wife, the stepmother, and the Mama Manya recalled with tears in her eyes was the sturdy woman with a bun on a faded sepia photograph that their father kept at the bottom of one of the drawers. Sometimes, Manya and Mike would remove and caress it, speaking of and seemingly tasting the delicious potato dumplings smothered in fried onions and sour cream and the thick cabbage soup and beet soup they ate in the kitchen on Division, but Stefa had nothing to add except to say that, as far as she was concerned, the new Mama's pierogis and *kapusnyak* and borscht

101

were also the best in the world. Her siblings' memories weren't her memories and Fall River and Narragansett Bay and its world-famous snails and the palatial brown house at the foot of Division Street and the gently sloping park where one could tumble and play all day long did not exist, at least as far as she was concerned.

There were many other memories Stefa couldn't share. For instance, Manya would tell her and Mike that their parents had come to the United States in 1910 and immediately headed for the Pennsylvania coal mines. What was Pennsylvania? Stefa used to think, while Mike just nodded sagely as if he knew just what that strange agglomeration of sounds represented. Yes, continued Manya, that's where they went, but Tato couldn't stand the harsh conditions in the mines, so he and Mama pulled up and headed for Fall River, because their friends who lived there said everybody was doing well and shoes were being worn out quickly and Tato could easily get a job as a shoemaker and make good money. And, besides, Fall River couldn't be any worse than living in some smelly, dirty, awful mining town where you had to work for ten or fifteen hours a day in a dank and dark coal mine chipping away at a wall of unyielding rock and inhaling black dust that made you cough.

It may have been just as well that Stefa couldn't share this memory, because it wasn't a real memory, but a story Manya stitched together from her parents' conversations with their Fall River friends. Their father had actually come to America in July of 1913 and he had headed straight for Fall River, having declared his profession on the ship's manifest of the Lützow as shoemaker; once there, he lived with a friend, Sylwester Demkowicz, also a shoemaker, who had left Przemyślany back in 1910. And their mother had come directly to Fall River in early 1914 and then Manya had been born in late 1914. Even if imagined, Manya's story was a great story and Stefa listened with wonder at her frail Tato's ability to hack away with a pick at a cliff and with admiration at her parents' fortitude and strength and determination to get to Fall River at any cost, because that's where she was to be born, even if she had no memories whatsoever of the place or the house.

The one-family house at the foot of the steep street that was named after somebody or something named Division was another memory Stefa could not share with Manya and Mike. That house was, Manya proudly insisted, *their* house, their very own house, just like the house they all lived in here, in Przemyślany, on ulica Pocztowa. See? Manya would say, we were rich and Tato had money and we all had nice clothes and wonderful shoes—and at that point Manya would show Stefa and Mike the photographs of the family in Fall River and instruct them to look closely at how pretty their dresses were and how handsome Mike looked in his sailor's suit and how distinguished Tato looked in his three-piece suit and ten-gallon hat. But, after Mama died, Manya would say, Tato sold the house and we packed up all our belongings and came here, to Przemyślany, which is now our home, even though it doesn't have Narragansett Bay and South Park and that wonderful Portuguese bakery with the delicious donuts Mama would buy me or the little stand that sold fried potato chips, which cost only one penny.

And it may have been just as well that Stefa couldn't share this memory of the house, because it, too, wasn't a real memory, but a story Manya must have imagined, in the manner, perhaps, that most memories are imagined. In reality, the family had lived in the brown house at the foot of Division for about three years in the early nineteen-twenties. It surely felt like theirs to Manya and, if it felt like theirs, it must have been theirs. But neither Manya nor Mike nor Stefa could possibly have known that their Tato had never bought or sold the house. He had been renting it all along, which made perfect sense, if you thought about it, since how could a newly arrived immigrant-shoemaker who sent his mother the money she used to buy or build the house on Pocztowa have had any left over for a down payment on a house in Fall River?

The death of Mama—the stout woman Stefa couldn't remember at all, no matter how hard she tried—was another memory she couldn't share with Manya or even Mike, who had an indistinct recollection of some of the sadness, black clothes, and wreaths at the cemetery, but not much else. But Manya remembered all the details: Mama's sudden illness, her confinement to bed, the stuffy room and her perpetually moist forehead, the day they took her to the hospital up the hill, the operation, and the terrible news, exactly one day after the large mirror in the living room crashed to the floor and broke into millions of little pieces that scattered across the entire floor, into all the corners, and even into the kitchen, that Mama had died. And then the long ride in the open cart, while the snow lashed their faces and the wind blew savagely and she froze but barely felt it, because she was so desperately sad that her beloved Mama, who kissed her and loved her and took her collecting snails and bought her donuts at the Portuguese bakery and cooked such magnificent cabbage soup and borscht and potato and cheese dumplings, was lying in a wooden box in some deep hole next to a fence and next to a railroad track far away from the city. And what worried Manya was that her mother would freeze in such a cold hole, unless her soul had had the good sense to leave immediately for Heaven, where it was surely warm and where she could wait for the children and Tato and bake to her heart's content. And this was the one memory it really was too bad Stefa couldn't share, because it was completely true to the facts as they unfolded in those funereal wintry days of 1922.

The other fact little Stefa could have known, but didn't, was that her name was given as Stella on her birth certificate and passport. Had she been able to read, she might have shared Manya's amazement when, one day, she glanced at Stefa's passport—it may have been on the boat going over—and noticed that her little sister had the wrong name. "So," she asked her father that same day, "is Stefa Stefania or Stella?" Tato was just as surprised as Manya when she showed him the passport. He examined the birth certificate, which he kept neatly folded in a brown leather case along with all

104

the other important family documents, produced a long whistle, and said, "I have no idea how this happened. Maybe the clerk in the city office where we registered Stefa's birth made the mistake. Maybe he had never heard of Stefania or maybe your Mama mispronounced the name, but there it is: Stella, not Stefa, even though"—and then he took Stefa in his arms—"you'll always be our beautiful little Stefa and we love you very much." And Manya embraced Stefa, too, while Mike, not quite understanding why some silly name required so much hugging and kissing, just stood to the side and looked quizzically at his father and sisters.

There were, of course, many other memories Stefa couldn't share with Manya, Mike, and Tato, but these two or three were probably the most important ones or, in any case, they were the most important ones for Manya and Mike.

There were also a few things Stefa couldn't know about Przemyślany or about the hard times they all lived in. She had no idea that there had just been a World War—and, truth to tell, neither did Manya or Mike, except perhaps from stories that, unlike stories about the Pennsylvania coal mines or the textile mills of Fall River, they couldn't really understand. Stefa could have no idea that a Great Depression would descend on the world and make life in Przemyślany desperately hard. She certainly didn't know that the train tracks that went through town and connected it with Lviv had been built a few years before the war. And she probably couldn't have imagined that, without the rail, visiting Lviv, which was so expensive that Tato could only raise his eyebrows at the price, would have been next to impossible. And she definitely couldn't have known—or, more exactly, even imagined—what lay in store for the town and its inhabitants in the years ahead: that within twenty to twenty-five years of her setting foot in Przemyślany's lazy streets, the town would become an inferno for everyone who lived there and that life would become a personal hell for her even before it became a hell for everyone else. And it was all because of that lanky young man with the sad eyes who came into her life abruptly and then, just as abruptly, was torn from it, just as one might tear off a corner of a newspaper in order to make an impromptu bookmark.

There isn't much to relate about Stefa's life before he arrived on the scene. Born in 1922, entered primary school around 1928 or 1929, and graduated in 1936. There was no money and too many kids and no prospects in Przemyślany and Mike hadn't yet left for America, so Tato's two sisters had a brilliant idea: Stefa should become apprenticed with a Polish seamstress they knew. She lived in Lviv on ulica Kochanowskiego and might be convinced to provide Stefa with room and board in exchange for her services, while Stefa could also enroll in sewing classes at a trade school and learn an excellent profession for a girl without a gymnasium degree. And, besides, she was pretty and Lviv was full of handsome young men with ambitions and good educations.

Stefa's sojourn in Lviv began in 1937 and lasted for about two years, until the Nazis and Soviets partitioned Poland for the fourth time and the seamstress began worrying about the future, the trade school encountered financial and political difficulties, and Tato said she'd better come home to the family. Even though Lviv was only a train ride away, it was still too far and they'd all feel better if Stefa returned to Pocztowa. Stefa didn't mind. Lviv meant being on her own and seeing and experiencing things she had never even known existed: from the fashionable shops to the elegant restaurants and cafés to the coquettish young ladies with their furs to the nattily attired gentlemen with their fedoras slung over one eye. But Lviv also meant fifteen-hour days and constant needle pricks and sore fingers and tired eyes and a back that never stopped hurting. She had seen and experienced enough and, besides, if you had no money, just seeing and experiencing from afar lost their allure after a while. Poland's destruction came just at the right time: it was time to go home. And it's just about then that Bohdan appeared and her life turned upside down.

How Bohdan got to Przemyślany is a story in itself, one that had absolutely nothing to do with Stefa, Mike, or Manya. Unlike the three siblings who were newcomers to the town and to the country where it was located, Bohdan was born and raised in an equally insignificant little town called Zbaraż, some one hundred kilometers east-southeast of Przemyślany and just a few kilometers north of Lviv's provincial urban cousin, Tarnopol, as the Poles and Jews would have called it, or Ternopil, as it was known to the Ukrainians. His exact date of birth is unimportant, although the year, 1915, is not, as it meant that, when he met Stefa in 1939, he was already twenty-four and had by then spent some five or six years in Polish prisons, while she was a mere seventeen, still a teenage girl with adolescent dreams of love and preposterous fantasies of never-ending happiness.

Bohdan's father was a gymnasium professor of Latin and ancient Greek: he believed in disciplining and, if necessary, applying the rod to the boy, who exhibited at a very early age a decided proclivity for climbing tall trees, eating the neighbors' sour cherries, pears, and apples, and feigning illness to avoid going to Sunday Mass. That was intolerable, of course, if only because it reflected poorly on the professor and his reputation as a demanding teacher. The boy came to fear his father—and, oddly enough, retained that fear even into adulthood—possibly because of the all too frequent encounters with the rod in the proverbial woodshed that stood between the house and, some twenty meters away, the stone walls of a massive fortress that had once housed Cossack leaders and their armies hundreds of years ago.

The ruins were among the boy's favorite places to play and to hide. Subterranean passageways extended into underground chambers that, alas, stored no riches, no skeletons, and no sabers, but that could, with only a little bit of effort, be imagined as containing all these marvelous objects. He and his friends spent hours exploring the passages, chambers, tunnels, and ruins. Bohdan invariably led the way, a flickering candle in his right hand and a pocket knife in his left. Elongated shadows and eerie caverns terrified his friends, but not him. Indeed, the only thing he feared in life was his father: his very presence, his physical appearance, and his spiritual domination. Naturally, as in most such family relationships, there was also a mother who loved him and a younger sister who adored him.

The house was full of books—in Polish, Ukrainian, German, Russian, as well as Latin and Greek—but Bohdan had little use for them. He read what he had to read. Once the assignment was complete, there was little point in poring over pages of print when there was so much to do outside, in the trees, among the ruins, on the streets. There is an irony here that will become strikingly apparent later in the story, when Bohdan's love of the outdoors eventually met its antithesis in years of incarceration. Obviously, the young boy could have had no clue of how fate would play such abominably cruel tricks on him at several stages of his life and decisively resolve the dialectic with a brutal synthesis involving unimaginable pain.

He did share two of his father's traits, however, and these were an inexhaustible pride and an indefatigable determination. His father applied both to his profession and was considered by his colleagues, if not necessarily by his students, to be an extraordinary pedagogue with an outstanding mind. Bohdan applied both traits to his relations with the world. His friends knew that an off-hand remark or a disrespectful glance, however brief, could elicit a shove in the chest or a punch in the nose. You did not, they knew, mess with Danchyk, the diminutive of Bohdan he favored, perhaps because it belied the reality—that he was a strong, powerful, and fearless boy—and deluded potential adversaries into thinking he was the push-over he decidedly was not.

The Jewish boys immediately understood that his external strength was evidence of internal fortitude and always greeted him respectfully and followed his lead in games of football. It was the Polish boys who viewed his self-confidence as an affront to their natural superiority and who sniggered and called him "*kabanie*".

108

They only did so when they outnumbered him by at least four to one and Bohdan was wise enough to understand his limitations and turn red, clench his fists, and walk by silently. But every time he heard that taunt, swine, he vowed to take revenge. Sooner or later, it would be his turn and then we'd see who would snigger on the streets as he walked past.

That time came in the summer of 1930, when Eastern Galicia burned for months and the black night sky turned red and yellow as towering fires consumed Polish property, everything from houses to barns to stacks of grain to wagons, and it seemed to everyone that a rebellion was in the works and that blood would soon flow. It did, in September, but it was mostly Ukrainian blood that flowed, after the Polish military and police descended on the towns and villages and "pacified" the population, arresting thousands in the process. Fifteen-year old Bohdan was one of them and he was subsequently convicted of arson. The eleven months in jail were a harsh introduction to a reality he had heard about but never seen, but they did nothing to dispel his belief that setting fire to Kolączkowski's property had been absolutely justified.

Two members of the underground Organization had asked him if he'd like to join and show his mettle by taking part in his first "action." "Of course," he said without hesitation. "What?" "Kolączkowski must be punished," they said. "He is organizing young Poles in paramilitary units and training them to fight against us. This is our land and they have no right to tell us how to run our affairs." The Organization had decided that Kolączkowski would be taught a lesson he'd never forget if they set fire to his house, a handsome two-story structure in the good part of town, where the best *cukernia* and the most elegant *restauracja* were located amid a few paved streets and sidewalks.

Bohdan was deemed crucial to the plan's success precisely because no one would pay attention to a young boy carrying a small package under his arm. His co-conspirators would stand at opposite ends of the street in which the house was located and warn him of approaching policemen by whistling. All Bohdan had to do was dash down a little path that divided Kolączkowski's building from his neighbor's, jump over the pleated fence, cross the garden without trampling the vegetables, and find the little veranda in the back. Then open the package, remove the jar with kerosene, sprinkle it on the veranda and door, and light a match. He should leave the same way he came and, as soon as the fire was visible, run to a neighbor, bang on his door, and shout "*Pożar!*" Sounding the alarm would establish his innocence. They would meet him near the tavern, where their colleagues would vouch that the young rapscallion had been drinking all evening. It was a bad plan, of course.

Kolączkowski's house lit up the night sky the color of pomegranates and Bohdan got away without any misadventures, but the police investigation identified him as the boy who warned the neighbors of the fire and arrived at the tavern later than he claimed. Less fortuitously, the neighbor noticed a suspiciously large black smear across Bohdan's forehead, which confirmed the procurator's charge that the boy, well known to the local police for his proclivity for fist fights with patriotic Polish youths, had been up to no good. The court found him guilty of arson and, considering his age, sentenced him to only one year in jail. Bohdan stood ramrod straight as the verdict was read and, although his mother cried and his father looked disappointed, he refrained from showing any emotion. If this is what the cause required, then so be it. He would, he decided, be ready to die for his country.

Prison proved to be an invaluable school for the boy. His cellmates were three young Ukrainians, all members of the Organization who had also been sentenced for arson or other anti-state activities. All three were in their twenties and had had ample experience in the underground. One knew how to make bombs: nothing terribly powerful, but sufficiently loud and destructive to remind the Polish occupiers that their rule would soon end. Another had been involved in several "expropriations" during which letter carriers or bank tellers were liberated of the money they were holding on behalf of the oppressive state. The third had run an illegal printing press and been responsible for pasting anti-Polish leaflets in embarrassing public places. The round-faced guards regularly beat all three, sometimes with nightsticks across their backs, sometimes with rubber truncheons across the soles of their feet. They agreed the latter technique was more painful. "I would never have believed that the sole can be such a sensitive place," one of them told Bohdan. "But don't worry, my young friend. They won't touch you because of your age." And, indeed, Bohdan left jail a far wiser and more knowledgeable nationalist with his back and soles and dignity fully intact.

There followed two lackluster years of gymnasium, during which time the boy, now a precocious young man, primarily occupied himself with organizational work in the underground. He had a gift for spotting talent and convincing potential members to join the Organization. Weekly meetings, usually organized around football games, bonfires, or swims in a nearby creek, focused on the repressive course of Polish policy and the threat posed by accommodationist Ukrainians who preferred reform to revolution. After a terrible famine devastated Soviet Ukraine and hundreds of refugees managed to drag their thin carcasses across the narrow river that served as the Polish-Soviet boundary and arrive, tired, hungry, desperate, and bedraggled, in Ternopil, the Soviet Union increasingly came to occupy the young nationalists' attention. The Organization was steadily growing, but everyone knew it consisted mostly of youngsters without any weapons or training. How could, Bohdan wondered, they possibly defeat two large states with formidable armies and ruthless police forces?

The assassination of Minister of the Interior Bronisław Pieracki in Warsaw on June 15, 1934 provided part of the answer. The wave of arrests that followed swept up Bohdan and thousands of others and, this time, he landed in a newly built concentration camp in the distant forests of marshy Polesie. Ukrainian nationalists formed about half the inmates; the others were Polish and Jewish communists who spoke glowingly of Stalin and denounced nationalism as a bourgeois deviation bordering on fascism. At first, the two sides didn't get along and catcalls, shoving, and even fistfights were not uncommon. But the harshness of the camp soon forged a commonality, not of spirit, but of hatred of the prison authorities and their lackeys, the guards. You had to run everywhere: from the bunk to the latrine, from the latrine to the washroom, from the washroom to the mess, from the mess to the work house or the fields, from the work house or the fields to the latrine—all day, every day, until all you could think of was running and all you could gnarl at was the guards and their truncheons.

Step out of line or fall out of file or arrive late or come early or make too much noise while slurping the greasy cabbage swill or dawdle too long in the latrine with your pants down or hold your face beneath the cold water for too long—and the curses would ensue and, before you could defend your head or dry your hands or lift your pants, the truncheons would be set in motion and your head and shoulders and chest and back and arms would be showered with blows that stopped only when you began running and escaped them. And then they would laugh—deep, heavy, offensive guffaws that emerged from within their well-fed guts—as they called you a swine and told you never to take it easy again, not unless you wanted more blows to your head or neck or shoulders or chest or back or arms.

None of these physical tribulations or emotional humiliations mattered to Bohdan. They were annoyances, but he knew he had the strength of both body and spirit to overcome them. No, what pushed him to the verge of despair was the blurring of days, the simultaneous compression and extension of time, and the resultant sensation that he lived in an endless no man's land, a place with no boundaries, no dimensions, and no future, present, or past. Was this what hell was like? How was he to live, whether for himself, his family, or his nation, when life was reduced to a never-ending repetition of petty details? How was he to struggle when there was nothing but emptiness to struggle against? Ultimately, existence itself became pointless and, when realization of that condition fully sank in, the easiest thing to do was to run and run and run without thinking or feeling anything.

It was Wlodzio Nakoneczny, a thirty-nine-year old womanizer and part-time pickpocket from Lviv, who saved him. He had been mistakenly arrested as an underground leader and, however much he assured the police that he couldn't possibly be the determined nationalist they had been hunting for months, they threw him in the camp along with all the other political swine. Whatever the circumstances, Wlodzio always had a silly grin on his face and, when he and Bohdan came to share a cell in 1935, the young nationalist initially thought the thief was mocking him. Bohdan was too apathetic to say anything or even care, but Wlodzio immediately engaged him in conversation and proceeded to relate off-color jokes that soon had the whole cell in stitches.

A few weeks later, when Wlodzio spent several days in the "hole," as the inmates called solitary confinement, he emerged with the same ridiculous grin and, upon seeing Bohdan, even winked. "I don't understand you," Bohdan said. "We are in a concentration camp and you act as if you were at a resort." Wlodzio's eyes twinkled. "I sing," he said, "but quietly, of course, and the singing sustains my humor and my sanity. You should try it." "I have no voice," Bohdan protested, but Wlodzio ignored him and went on: "I sing an American song I heard somewhere, but you can sing anything you like. And I sing it over and over in my head, whether I am running or shitting or being beaten by one of those Polish brutes or"—he couldn't resist grinning—"one of my girlfriends. I forget everything and hear only the words and the sounds as they course through my head. After I repeat them long enough, they enter my body and soul and then the world could end as far as I'm concerned: I wouldn't notice a thing. Well, maybe a good lay." And then Wlodzio sang a song Bohdan had never heard before and whose words he couldn't understand. "The refrain," Bohdan said, "what does the refrain mean: 'Smo'getsinyorize'?" Wlodzio laughed. "I don't know. I don't understand English!" Bohdan laughed, too, and then he said: "I like the melody. Can you teach me the words or just the refrain?" Wlodzio did, which was fortunate, for the next time he landed in solitary, he died. The prison authorities said it was a burst appendix; the prisoners decided it had to be murder.

Not much happened in the camp during the four years Bohdan spent there. The daily routine never varied and dirt, filth, vermin, and hunger were his constant companions. Every once in a while some inmate tried to commit suicide; every once in a while he succeeded. Fist fights were still a regular occurrence, but they became more desultory, more ritualized, as the prisoners lacked the physical strength to exchange serious body blows. Illnesses were the order of the day: toothaches, colds, diarrhea, and respiratory diseases were most common. As the inmates came to understand the ins and outs of the daily routine, however, they also discovered how they could exchange notes, acquire cigarettes and other contraband, and engage in genuine discussions. Both nationalists and communists formed amorphous groups that would emerge as if by accident and dissolve wordlessly whenever a guard approached. The discussions would continue at night and, when the wind was still and the crickets were asleep, the building resounded with a barely audible roar: the whisperings of hundreds of men. The communists refined their communist beliefs, while the nationalists refined their nationalist beliefs. Both sets of prisoners entered the camp as individuals with few contacts and few friends, but they quickly acquired networks of trustworthy comrades who would lay down their lives for them and the cause.

Informers were a plague on everyone. They were either too evasive or too bold or too insistent in their conversations with the others. Real revolutionaries had all the time in the world, whether to listen to their interlocutors, to dream of the future, or to plan their revenge. Informers appeared to have too little time and were always in a hurry to find out irrelevant details about the movement or the comrades. When spies were identified, they would usually be found beaten and bloody in the shower room, with bars of yellow soap stuffed into their mouths. Sometimes they'd be stuffed into the filthy pits beneath the latrines. When it came to punishing informers, the nationalists and communists could count on each other for help: ideological battles would cease, a curious solidarity would emerge, and sentences would be meted out efficiently to the guilty.

By the time he was released in early 1938, Bohdan had acquired a consummate understanding of the two ideologies and movements that opposed the Polish state with equal vigor. He emerged into the daylight an even more implacable believer in the rightness of the cause. He had also acquired an indifference to physical and mental pain. It wasn't heroism, although he wished it were. It was, quite simply, the indifference Wlodzio had taught him: an indifference to the world and its tribulations that shaded into a near-religious devotion to the only things that mattered to Bohdan, the ideas or ideals that gave his life meaning and, thus, endowed him with spiritual gratification. "Smo'getsinyorize" and Ukraine were all that really mattered.

The authorities forbade Bohdan to settle in Zbaraż: it was too close to the Soviet border and flight was deemed a risk. A stupid rule, Bohdan thought, as east is the last place in the world he would go. His mother and sister cried, happy that he had finally been released and sad that he would not be coming home. His father, by then retired, adjusted the glasses on his nose when he heard the news and said the boy would be fine. The Organization instructed Bohdan to move to Przemyślany, a small town near Lviv that could use a good organizer. The local comrades met him with open arms, found him a room and a job, and introduced him to the network.

A few months later, in mid-1938, he was arrested again and sentenced to five years for anti-state activity. This time he was incarcerated in a fetid cell in the notorious prison on ulica Łąckiego in Lviv. The beatings and torture began almost immediately and continued for the duration of his imprisonment. He was used to truncheons, fists, brass knuckles, and other such implements. He had also experienced the intense pain of having the soles of his feet beaten with a piece of hard rubber. The humiliation of defecating under a guard's watchful gaze and of having only a few seconds to take a cold shower was also bearable, especially as he found strength in intoning "Smo'getsinyorize." His fortitude came to be tested and his will was almost broken when the guards wrapped him tightly in a wet blanket and watched it dry: unlike beatings, which were localized, this technique produced an intense pain throughout his entire body. When every nerve ending was screaming for the torture to stop, it took every ounce of will and defiance to continue muttering "smo'getsinyorize, smo'getsinyorize, smo'getsinyorize, smo'getsinyorize" and not beg for them to stop, for Christ's sake, to stop and please let him go.

But the very worst was being taken atop a platform three meters above the ground, bound to a plank, and dropped. The fall lasted a second and the pain that shot through and reverberated in his head and chest and neck and arms and legs made him bite his lips until they bled, but the truly terrifying part came in the second or two just before the plank was tipped over. It was then, standing at the brink of the void and knowing full well that excruciating pain would soon follow, that he even prayed and interspersed God's holy name within the magic formula that enabled him to survive so many depredations: "Smo'getsinyorize, o, God, smo'getsinyorize, o, my Lord, smo'getsinyorize, Jesus, smo'getsinyorize, o, my God!"

How many times did he endure the plank? Once a week, sometimes twice, for several months, during which time the hollow sound of the board's striking the cement floor rattled constantly in his head and even his dreams reenacted his falling and hitting the rough concrete over and over again. They almost broke him this time, but Bohdan was able to save himself by retreating into a trance-like passivity that eventually persuaded his torturers that no amount of wet blankets or plank droppings would destroy him. In time, they abandoned the refined tortures and simply beat and humiliated him, so as to remind him, lest he forgot, that he was the vermin and they were the masters.

Who knows whether Bohdan would have survived his sentence? At some point, no matter how strong one's will to live, an emaciated body ceases to function and death ensues. His skeletal frame suggested his end was near, but then the miraculous happened: Germany and the Soviet Union destroyed Poland. The prisons were opened and all the prisoners were set free. Bohdan happened to be sitting in a corner of his cell when his friends came for him. They washed and fed him and let him sleep in a clean bed for days. Then they boarded a train festooned with Soviet flags and hammers and sickles for Przemyślany.

It was hard to believe that the hated Polish state was no more. Soviet military men, their chests thrust forward and their arms swinging rhythmically, paraded along the streets of Lviv. Policemen and tram operators all wore Soviet insignia. Fervent communist marching songs were piped in over the loudspeakers at the train station and posters of muscular Russian workers embracing emaciated Ukrainian peasants and kissing them squarely on the mouth adorned buildings and fences. The Poles walked with their heads down, the Jews had smiles on their faces, and the Ukrainians seemed confused, uncertain about the Soviet Ukrainian reality that had descended on them like a fog. Was it Soviet? Was it Ukrainian? Or was it both? And, if it were, how could it be both? The sun was shining brightly and there were too many people, far too many people, on the platform and they were all talking and laughing and hurrying. Bohdan felt confused. The world and his life had turned upside down while he had been in prison. It was at this time that Stefa returned home and would change his life even more.

She sat in the third-class compartment on an unyielding wooden bench and gazed out the streaked window at the ripe green trees whizzing past her. She was going home. After two years of living with that seamstress in Lviv, after two years of attending night school, after two years of living outside the confines of her family, she was returning to the little house on Pocztowa, to her father and his wife and their children. She had kissed Mike good-bye as he boarded the train for Germany. She had met with Manya and Fanka every few months and they had strolled along the city's fashionable streets and eaten cake and drunk tea. But mostly she had sewn and cut cloth and sewn and cut cloth in an endless repetition that merged all days and reduced infinity to a second and made seconds seem infinite. Had she really spent two years in Lviv? Sometimes, they felt more like two days or two thousand years. In any case, that period of her life was over and she was going home.

The trees assumed distinct shapes, the train decelerated, and, as she recognized the familiar station, an extended screech assaulted her ears. Outside, amid the red banners and posters of a benevolent Stalin, she saw Tato, Manya, and young Slavko. They were peering intently at the train cars and looking for her. She collected her cardboard suitcase and coat and hat and, after restraining her impatience in the slow crawl toward the exit, bounded down the iron stairs and almost fell into her father's surprised arms. Slavko took her things and Manya showered her with kisses and, with Slavko leading the way and Manya and Tato holding her arms, they made their way up linden alley, turned left just before Mickiewicz Street, and were soon home. More kisses and embraces followed, small glasses of a sticky sweet liqueur were raised to her health, and then the family sat down to eat at a table covered with an unusually large assortment of dumplings, stuffed cabbage, and meatloaf. As she chewed on the pierogis and felt the cheese and dough dissolve in her mouth, Stefa knew she was home.

That night, she slept fitfully, waking what seemed like every few minutes. A popular Polish song she had often heard in Lviv kept recurring in her thoughts: *"Kamień na kamieniu, na kamieniu kamień, a na tym kamieniu jeszcze jeden kamień." There's a stone on the stone, and on the stone there's a stone, and on that stone is yet another stone.* When she awoke in the morning, before the sun rose, she had no idea what these words could possibly mean and felt anxious. In all likelihood, they signified nothing. Nonsense, after all, was nonsense. Or were they a premonition of something? That day, she asked Manya if the lyrics made any sense to her. Manya thought for a minute and then her dark eyes lit up. "Do you know how the rest of the song goes? *'Kamień na kamieniu, nad kamieniem woda, jak kamień przepłynie to będziesz ty moją'*! It's a good sign: *There's a stone on the stone, and on the stone there's water, and when it flows past the stone you'll be mine.* See, Stefa? You're going to meet the love of your life!"

They met at the annual pre-Lenten ball. A local band consisting of three gray-haired men in badly pressed tuxedoes and wilted bow ties—an accordionist, a violinist, and a drummer—was playing fox trots and waltzes and it was only after the girls complained that the drummer quickened the beat and the band took up some modern dances. Stefa knew the steps well, having learned them in Lviv, and was very much in demand by all the boys who remembered her as the skinny girl who had left for the big city a few years ago. Here was a modern woman and a beauty at that. Bohdan came late. He hadn't wanted to go: such frivolous entertainment seemed inappropriate while Ukraine was fighting for her survival. And, besides, he had no suit, only a pair of rumpled pants that refused to be ironed and a worn-out jacket with improvised elbow patches. He could borrow a shirt and tie, but, what with his height, none of his friends' better suits fit him.

When he stepped into the hall, Bohdan's eyes immediately fixated on the auburn-haired girl gliding along the dance floor like a cat one minute and flapping her elbows like a bird the next. He even stopped humming "smo'getsinyorize" and waited for the band to take a break. The girl sat at a table where a friend of his, Manya, was sipping punch and chatting with an admirer. He crossed the room and greeted her. "This is Ostap," she said, "and this is my sister, Stefa. The two of you are newcomers: did you know that? Stefa's just come home from Lviv and Bohdan has come to us from"— and she paused. "Prison," he promptly said. "Four and a half years."

And then, after he occupied the chair next to Stefa's, the first thing he said to her was: "I will marry you and you will be my wife." Stefa blushed and said nothing. He was tall and strong and she liked his determination. Every man should be like that. But it was clear from his face that he had been in jail for a long time: his skin was sallow and his eyes resembled puddles in the snow. He moved his hands slowly but deliberately and he neither smoked nor drank. He didn't dance and that was a great disappointment, but Stefa, much to her surprise, didn't mind sitting out the remainder of the evening.

When the ball was over, he asked if he could walk her home and she said yes. When they turned into Pocztowa and stood before the house, Bohdan squeezed Stefa's hand and said good-bye. "When will I see you again?" she said. "For the rest of your life," he answered, absurdly proud of his choice of melodramatic words. As he walked home and thought of her, it was probably inevitable that he would begin humming "smo'getsinyorize." The tune and the sounds had become a habit and, although they reminded him of his terrible days in the camp, they also assured him of his survival and his strength. He would, he decided, have to marry her as soon as possible. Who knew what the future would bring? Who knew what surprises fate had in store for them?

The marriage took place on a cloudless day in August of 1940 and it was Father Kowcz who, doubtless unsuspecting that he would become a martyr in a few short years, sanctified their exchange of vows. Stefa's parents liked the boy and admired his courage and patriotism, but were worried he might soon land in jail again. What would Stefa do then? Manya said it would be good to have another brother. Although Bohdan was quite unlike Mykhasko in appearance, they both had, as she put it, sensitive souls. Stefa agreed with her sister and dismissed her father's concerns. "There is no more Poland," she said, "so who's to arrest him?" The couple moved into a spare room in an aunt's house. Stefa stayed at home and helped with the household, while Bohdan began working as an inspector for a Soviet agricultural agency. The job was ideal. It required that he travel to the surrounding villages and speak to the peasants about their crops and livestock: What were they growing? How many animals did they have? How much could they sell to the state? How much would they sell?

At the same time, he could continue agitating on behalf of the Organization. The goal was to establish a solid network of village supporters who would provide information on Soviet troop and police movements, distribute clandestine literature and leaflets, and eventually join the uprising. A war between Hitler and Stalin was inevitable and, when it broke out, Ukraine would finally have a chance to be free. The Organization would be ready, all the more so as, after the initial euphoria of liberation by the Soviets, the NKVD had begun arresting community leaders and suspected nationalists and the popular mood had become uniformly and unremittingly anti-Soviet.

Bohdan knew he was under surveillance. Any one of his coworkers could be an informer and the heads of the village councils he met with certainly reported on him to the secret police. Although his movements were easy enough to follow, the NKVD couldn't pursue him everywhere and it certainly couldn't keep track of everybody he met with, particularly in the outlying villages. The strictest conspiracy was therefore imperative and that meant keeping Stefa, Manya, and the rest of his in-laws in the dark. They probably suspected anyway. How could they not expect a patriot and hardened political prisoner to return to his old ways?

Several times in 1940, he traveled to Lviv for meetings of the Organization. The train was out of the question, so he'd leave the house as soon as it turned dark and, hoping for a moonless sky, walk to the edge of town where a comrade would be waiting for him with a wagon loaded with hay or vegetables. Bohdan would burrow underneath and lie there for the two to three hours it took to reach the outskirts of the city. There he'd be met by another colleague and the two would walk on foot, avoiding the streets and wending their way through the backyards, to the assigned meeting place. Ten to fifteen members of the Organization would assemble in some sympathizer's house, draw the curtains as tightly as possible, light a candle, and discuss their plans in whispers.

There were reliable reports of German troops being deployed to the west. Although the tone of official propaganda suggested that the Soviet-Nazi alliance was unbreakable, it was clear that Hitler was preparing an attack. War had already broken out in France. Russia would be next, perhaps this year, perhaps next, at the very latest. And when war came, the Organization would initiate a massive uprising against the retreating Soviets and seize control of Ukrainian territory before the Nazis swept in. "Organize your networks," the leader of the cell said, "acquire weapons, train your cadres, and wait for our signal. Timing will be essential. When war breaks out, the uprising must begin everywhere at the same time." The meetings usually ended after two hours and Bohdan would crawl back into bed by daybreak, his heart racing from the journey and the heated exchanges.

In a case of exceptionally bad timing, Stefa became pregnant in April 1941, just two months before Hitler launched Operation Barbarossa against the Soviet Union. Their families were delighted at the wonderful news and Bohdan, now a married man and a father-to-be, noticed he no longer feared his father. Oddly, six years in jail and the maturity he had acquired as a result of his daily confrontations with death hadn't had this effect, but, as soon as he burst into the family house in Zbaraż and announced the news of Stefa's pregnancy, he realized he had finally become his father's equal. The fear had vanished and the need for approbation was gone. He had, at that very moment, become a man. It was definitely going to be a boy, he said, and his name would be Lev and he would be a great patriot like his father. Stefa would have preferred Ivan, after her father, but she knew better than to argue with her husband when he made up his mind.

It was in mid-June that Bohdan decided Stefa should spend the summer with his parents. They had a large house, she'd have a room of her own, and she could spend the day resting in the cool shade of the luxuriant garden in the back. This time, Stefa decided to put her foot down and said no. All her friends and family were in Przemyślany and she knew no one in Zbaraż; moreover, her parents and aunts also had gardens. But Bohdan insisted: her place was with his family and it was his decision to make. They quarreled and remained unreconciled when she boarded the train to Ternopil on June 14 and he followed with her cardboard suitcase. He said nothing, she said nothing, and they didn't even kiss after he deposited the suitcase on the shelf above her seat. And when the train rolled out of the station, she noticed out of the corner of her eye that he had already left. So be it, she thought. He'll come to regret it. The first few days in Zbaraż were awkward for everyone, but Stefa quickly became good friends with Bohdan's sister and also found a common language with her mother-in-law. Within a week she was happy she had bowed to Bohdan's will, even though he could be as stubborn as an ox and as infuriating as a child.

German troops launched their Blitzkrieg on June 22. Bohdan decided he needed a haircut before visiting Stefa next weekend. He went to the barbershop owned by Moishe Nudelman or Pan Moszko as everyone called him. Pan Moszko asked him if he'd like a shave, but Bohdan said a trim would be just fine. Moszko carefully placed the crisply ironed white sheet on Bohdan's chest and shoulders and tied the corners behind his neck. His client was a young man, but the skin on his face and neck was tough and worn, like that of an old man, and it had tiny scars. "Have you ever considered using a cream for your face?" he asked. "It's very fashionable in Warszawa, Kraków, and Lwów." Bohdan laughed. "Me? But you know what, Pan Moszko? Give me a shave, after all." He had shaved that morning, but he liked the feel of the lather as it was applied to his face and the sound of the wooden brush knocking against the sides of the porcelain shaving mug and of the razor flitting across the taut leather strap. Pan Moszko grabbed the mug, poured some water into it, took the particularly soft brush he knew Pan Bohdan liked so much, and began preparing the lather. A few minutes later, Bohdan's face was covered with white foam and he leaned back in the chair and closed his eyes. "Smo'getsinyorize, smo'getsinyorize, smo'getsinyorize, smo'getsinyorize," he thought. His wife was with his family in Zbaraż and he was getting a close shave, even though he didn't need one. Life was good. "Smo'getsinyorize, smo'getsinyorize, smo'getsinyorize, smo'getsinyorize."

It was at precisely that moment that the door to the shop was thrown open and Bohdan heard the sound of heavy boots and the barking of commands in Russian. As he opened his eyes, someone tore the sheet from his neck and brusquely ordered him to get up from the chair. It was the NKVD. He wiped the foam from his face with his sleeve before they placed cuffs on his hands and led him away. They marched down ulica Mickiewicza to the prison and, as they passed Pocztowa, Manya happened to be standing on the corner talking to one of her Polish cousins. She turned white upon seeing Bohdan and immediately ran home to tell Tato the terrible news. When word of Bohdan's arrest reached Zbaraż next day, his mother read the telegram and fainted. Upon recovering, she murmured darkly: "We'll never see him again." Stefa and Bohdan's sister assured her he'd be out soon, that he had survived three stints in jail and would survive a fourth, but the old woman remained adamant and would not be swayed. No one slept well that night, either in Zbaraż or in Przemyślany.

There were twenty-one other men in the basement jail. Most were from the town, a few were from nearby villages, and all were suspected of having ties to the underground. Bohdan knew them all, either as comrades in the struggle or as friends who, he was surprised to learn, were also fellow nationalists. There were five or six men to a cell designed to accommodate two. The bunks had been removed to make more room and the men had to sit and sleep on the concrete floor. A dented iron pail stood in one corner, just below the small window, and it served as the collective toilet. The days were hot and, since ventilation was minimal and the guards purposely emptied the pails every other day, the stench was overpowering. Meals consisted of a greasy cabbage soup and a piece of oily gray bread. By the third day, the unwashed men began to stink as well and became less sensitive to the smell emanating from the pail.

Except for the times they were taken out individually and interrogated, they spent the days talking. The war they awaited had begun and Hitler's Germany was sure to defeat Stalin's Russia. Soviet power would be swept away and a free Ukrainian state would rise from the ashes. Would the Germans accept it? They would have no choice if they hoped to march on Moscow. More important, as the Wehrmacht seeped into the vast Russian spaces, the Ukrainians would establish their own administration, their own armed forces, their own police, and their own system of justice. Collaborators would be punished and minorities would have to declare their unconditional loyalty to the new masters of the land. And what if the Germans refused to accept Ukrainian independence? That was unthinkable. They'd have to be mad to sabotage their own war effort. Could the Organization lead the way? It had to; there was no alternative. And what of it didn't? That, too, was unthinkable.

Invariably, discussions of grand strategy quickly turned to their own fates. Here they were, in jail, while outside a momentous struggle was taking place and the German Wehrmacht was inflicting a humiliating defeat on the ragtag Red Army. Sooner or later, the Russians would have to withdraw. What, then, would happen to them, the prisoners? It was rumored that they'd be evacuated to the east. But why would the Soviets expend scarce rail capacity on moving enemies of the people? There were also rumors that they'd be released, perhaps as a gesture of good faith to the local population. But since when did the Soviet secret police concern itself with such niceties? There were also suspicions that they would all be killed. And why not? They were enemies and they couldn't be freed and they couldn't be evacuated. What else were the Russians to do but eliminate them with quick bullets to their heads? The men knew the third option was most likely, indeed, certain, but in their discussions they always returned to the other two and, perhaps in a sign of the desperate hope that accompanies the certainty of extinction, devoted far more time to them than to the third, which they treated as an afterthought. At night, as they all slept or pretended to sleep, whispers could be heard in the cells and everyone pretended not to hear. They were, of course, praying.

Interrogations were routine, even polite. Bohdan expected the NKVD to apply the methods he had experienced in Polish jails, but the Soviet secret police only inquired about his activities and his contacts. They appeared to know everything about him, but they obviously didn't know just how large and ramified the underground was. And they didn't have much information about the movement in the countryside. He told them only what he believed they already knew, expansively describing his introduction to the Organization, his arson-related activities in 1930, and his stints in the prisons and detention camp. They smiled and he smiled back and he realized after two such sessions that there was an oddly perfunctory quality to the conversations. It was almost as if the notorious secret police was biding its time and didn't really care what he had to say. The other inmates confirmed that their experiences were similar.

By the seventh day of their imprisonment, one of the inmates in Bohdan's cell, a peasant boy by the name of Mykola, broke down. The sun shone with a brightness and heat that transformed the cells into steam baths. They sat with their eyes half-closed. Breathing consisted of short, loud gasps and sweat rolled down faces, chests, hands, and fingers. Even their fingernails were wet. There was no talking and no whispering. The pail released a stench that clung to their skin and penetrated their pores and attached itself to their tongues and eyeballs. Suddenly, Mykola exploded in paroxysms of tears accompanied by a low moan that metamorphosed into high-pitched shrieks: "I want to live! I want to live! I want to live!" The others watched desultorily, almost with indifference. There was nothing for them to do. There was no way to help Mykola or

126

alleviate his pain. There was no way to stem his tears. Two of them placed their hands over their ears, while the others, Bohdan included, just watched as Mykola's hopeless outbursts lost in intensity and, after several hours, ceased altogether. The poor boy slumped against the wall with his head a few centimeters from the pail. Bohdan got to his knees and moved the receptacle. Let him rest in peace, he thought.

The eighth day of their imprisonment fell on June 30 and it proved to be decisive, indeed, fatal. They suspected something was amiss when the guards failed to bring anything to eat. It was also the day on which the pail was to be emptied and it wasn't. Instead, all day long they heard a continual movement of people, dogs, and machines accompanied by shouting, barking, and the clicking of heels along the stone-floored corridors. Motors were ignited and turned off. Heavy objects fell or appeared to be pushed or pulled. The pungent smell of burning paper filled the air. It was clear that the Russians were preparing to evacuate the prison and the town. What would happen to them? Perhaps, someone suggested, they'll just leave us in our cells? The Germans must be near and every second counts: the Russians would save their skins and they, the prisoners, would be left behind for the Germans to do with as they pleased. That made sense, someone else said. There were only twenty-two of us and how could we possibly affect the outcome of the war? The Russians would run while the running was good and to hell with the nationalists. Bohdan said nothing. He knew they wouldn't survive the night, which is when the NKVD preferred to do its dirty work. There was nothing to say or think but "smo'getsinyorize."

The killings began at ten o'clock at night. At first, the inmates heard what appeared to be trucks being parked near the prison with their motors running. A few minutes later, guards entered each cell and bound the prisoners' hands behind their backs with wire. Mykola fainted, while the others were thrown to the hard floor and their feet were tied with wire as well. Why their feet? Bohdan wondered. It obviously meant the NKVD planned to kill them here, in the cells, and not line them up before a pit and fire bullets through their skulls. Shouts, protestations, prayers, screams, and wailings arose from within the cells, forming a cacophony of inhuman sounds that made him think of an abattoir. They would be slaughtered like animals. Two of his cellmates wet their pants and their urine crept in rivulets along the concrete floor. Mykola lay quietly and stared at the wall. Bohdan said, "Well, comrades, we always said we would gladly give our lives for the cause," and immediately regretted lapsing into heroic pathos. They all knew what awaited them. They knew as well just why they were being killed. There was no point in spouting cheap sentiments that did nothing to change the fact of impending doom. Sure, Ukraine would live, even if they died. Sure, Ukraine would possibly live precisely because they died. But who could deny that it would be better if Ukraine could live and they could live?

Bohdan shut his eyes and tried to imagine Stefa in his parents' home. They had stupidly quarreled a week ago and he had stormed away from the train without saying good-bye to his young wife. He had begun castigating himself for his ridiculous stubbornness as soon as he heard the train pull out of the station. And now he'd never have the opportunity to kiss her warm cheeks again and pull her close to his breast. How thin she was. How delicate. How naturally she fit in his embrace. He had been right to have fallen in love immediately upon seeing her. Then again, what choice did he have? It was his fate to love and marry Stefa, just as, alas, it was his fate to die for his country with his feet and hands tied like a swine. When would the killing begin? He imagined the NKVD agents entering each cell and pointing their revolvers at the prisoners' heads and pulling the triggers. The blasts would reverberate throughout the basement and the shouts and screams and wailings and shootings would create an impenetrable din that would subside, then stop, as the killers went from cell to cell. Would their cell be first or last? It didn't matter, not ultimately of course, but he knew he'd prefer to be first. He could cope with his own fears, but listening to the pathetic pleadings of his comrades was more than his nerves could bear.

The Soviets began with their cell. But, contrary to his hope that several fast bullets would be unloaded efficiently into their heads, the secret police had other plans. He was the most senior member of the underground. He was the veteran. He was the one who, evidently, inspired the others. Before shooting them, they would break him and make him squeal for mercy. The filthy nationalists should know, even if just before dying, that there was no escaping the long hand of proletarian justice. They would be eliminated, but, far worse, they would be humiliated. When their turn for the bullet came, they would cringe like dogs fearful of receiving another blow from their master. They claimed to be heroes. They said they wanted to die like heroes. They would die like cockroaches.

Two slight policemen entered. Both had revolvers in their holsters, but both also carried ominous knives that glistened even in the bad light of the cell. "You," they pointed at Bohdan, "you, the hero. We have a surprise for you, esteemed comrade." They laughed. "You will have the opportunity to show your friends just how heroic you really are." What would they do? Bohdan thought. What should he do? Remain silent or show his defiance? "*Slava Ukraini!*" he shouted impulsively. "Glory to Ukraine!" They laughed: "Excellent—*otlichno*! We'll show you just how glorious you and your Ukraine really are." One of them knelt next to Bohdan and tore open his shirt and lowered his pants, exposing his pale body to the night. The other took the pail and poured the excrement over Bohdan's face. When the filth had run off to the side, he shouted "*Slava Ukraini!*" Again they laughed.

The agent dropped the pail and placed his heavy boot on Bohdan's face. His comrade brandished a knife and, with one motion and surgeon-like precision, removed Bohdan's genitals. "Go ahead," the agent said as he removed his boot, "go ahead and praise your beloved Ukraine. Go ahead and say it: *Slava Ukraini*. What's the matter, comrade? Are you distracted?" Shocked, stunned, and bewildered, Bohdan gasped for breath and shouted: "Smo'getsinyorize!" "What?" screamed the agent. "What was that? Are you laughing at Soviet power? We'll teach you to laugh at Soviet power!" He inserted the tip of the blade into Bohdan's groin and slid it across his stomach, across his chest, up his neck, and over his chin, stopping just below his lower lip. "You talk too much," he growled and, grabbing Bohdan's dry tongue with his left hand, detached it with the same deftness as before. "Go ahead," said the other policeman, "say it: *Slava Ukraini*. And you," he turned to the other prisoners, "do any of you want to sing?" He removed his revolver from the holster, inserted it into Bohdan's gurgling mouth, and pulled the trigger. "Any other heroes?" The others were silent as the two agents proceeded to fire single shots into their expectant skulls.

As the prisoners were being eliminated, three agents dug a pit in the back of the building. When everyone's work was done, the group shared a bottle of vodka and carried out the corpses. "Dump the hero first," someone suggested and they dropped what remained of Bohdan's bloody body into the hole. When all the bodies lay in the pit, they covered it with warm earth, patted the ground with their shovels, and boarded the trucks. The Germans were only a few kilometers away and it was high time to retreat. The trucks rumbled east just before the sun rose and the residents of the town encountered what some later said was an unusually eerie stillness that portended nothing good.

Stefa learned of Bohdan's death on July 1, just a few days before her twentieth birthday. The telegram came at about twelve noon and, when Bohdan's sister opened the door and saw the mailman, she knew immediately that he was bringing bad tidings. She tore open the envelope and read: "Bohdan dead. Manya." Her mother appeared at the door and grabbed the paper and turned white. Then Stefa inquired from the garden: "Who is it?" Mother and daughter found her sitting under the apple tree on a wooden bench constructed by Bohdan when he was still a teenager. The looks on their faces told her everything and, seemingly without emotion, she stated: "I have to go home and bury him." As she rose from the bench, she did a small pirouette and slumped to the ground. The two women carried her into the house and laid her on the sofa. "There's a train tomorrow morning," the mother said quietly. "You pack her things, while I'll take care of her." That night, no one slept. They sat in the kitchen drinking tea and watched the candle flicker and grow smaller.

Just before daybreak they left the house. Bohdan's father took the three women to Ternopil and, despite the masses of Soviet soldiers milling about the station waiting to be evacuated, they were able, after five hours in a stuffy waiting room, to catch a short train to Lviv. There, too, the station resounded with the shouts and shoves of thousands of people hoping to go somewhere. All semblance of order had disappeared and the three women had to push their way to the ticket window for another five hours. There were no trains to Przemyślany that day or the next, so they booked second-class seats for the day after and retired to the home of friends. The red banners and posters of Stalin had all disappeared and in their stead hastily made blue-and-yellow Ukrainian flags festooned windows and balconies. Smartly dressed German soldiers sporting shiny rifles and helmets sauntered along the streets, flaunting their authority in the same manner as their Soviet predecessors had done two years earlier.

Pedestrians were obviously on edge, avoiding eye contact and smiles and seeming to be in a great hurry. Their friends lived in the center, not far from the mayor's office, and they told them about the hundreds of rotting corpses that had been discovered in the city's godforsaken jails. Stefa broke down and began weeping upon hearing the news. There, apparently, thousands more throughout Galicia. And many of the bodies had been tortured before being shot. "Why would the Russians do that?" Bohdan's mother asked. "They had so little time to flee before the Germans came." "The Jews helped them," someone said. "The Jews run the NKVD. They have always hated us and now they've finally had their

131

chance to take revenge. But we'll pay them back." "Let's go home," Stefa pleaded, "please, let's go home as soon as possible." "It's the same everywhere," someone else said, "tortured bodies and rotting corpses everywhere. It's the Apocalypse." The sickly sweet smell of decomposing bodies hung above the city and clung to its walls.

The train to Przemyślany was already full of dull-eyed passengers when it slid into Lviv station; the three women had to push their way inside. There were up to ten people in compartments intended for six and the second-class wagons were packed with gloomy soldiers and tired peasants with enormous bundles stuffed onto the narrow racks, where they hung precariously like ominous storm clouds. The pungent smell of cheap tobacco, garlic, onions, homebrewed vodka, and sweat permeated the air and, even though the windows were open and a hot breeze blew in, the effect was like that of a sauna that burned rancid refuse to produce steam. Bohdan's determined mother elbowed her way to their compartment, but every centimeter of seating and standing space was already occupied by moist, jostling bodies. It was obvious that they would be unable to wrench their seats from the people who held them. "It's only ninety minutes," she said. "We'll survive this ordeal." "I think I'm going to faint," Stefa murmured, her eyes half-closed and her head lilting, but Bohdan's mother gently slapped her across her cheek and she remained conscious.

The train stopped every few minutes and, on several occasions, remained motionless for as long as half an hour. It's the troop transport trains, someone said. They have priority and we have to wait until they can let us through. Standing in the stifling heat, with unyielding bodies squeezing her on all sides and with pearls of sticky sweat trickling down her back and arms and nose, was bearable. Waiting for the train to resume moving was not. Stefa had to get home as quickly as possible; she had to bury her husband of two years: instead, she was standing and waiting and standing and waiting—for what? When the train finally lurched forward and the lumpy bodies jumped backward, her hopes grew until, inevitably, the screeching of steel on steel announced another interminable wait. The bursts of gunfire and the sound of exploding shells were almost a welcome distraction. The Russians were in full retreat, someone said, and the Germans wouldn't bomb civilian targets. Their train would be safe, unless the perfidious Russians had placed explosives along the tracks. But Stefa's thoughts didn't linger on such eventualities: she had a husband to bury and they were stuck in a train. Any movement was a godsend.

They finally straggled into Przemyślany six hours after leaving Lviv. The sun was already setting. A bright red orb nestled just above the rolling hills, it cast blinding rays on Tato and Manya, who were waiting impatiently on the platform. The train eased into the station and stopped, emitting cumulous clouds of steam and glowing eerily in the bloody sun. Bohdan's mother led the way and the three women squirmed through the crowd and emerged, their clothes disheveled and their faces pale, at the top of the stairs, where they paused to take a deep breath. Manya was the first to espy them and, waving her white handkerchief, shouted, "Stefa! Stefa! Here we are! Here we are!" Tears, embraces, and vague assurances followed and then the group set out along the famous street lined with luscious linden trees. Her father wanted to turn left before they reached the prison and head for home along the back ways, but Stefa insisted they look at the building. They paused in front of it and she asked: "Where is his body?" "They've all been buried," Tato answered, "in a common heroes' grave." "So I came too late?" Stefa said. "I can't even say good-bye to his corpse?" "They had to," Manya continued, "because of the heat. We said good-bye for you, Stefa." "Then," said Stefa, "let's go to the cemetery: I want to see the grave." And she began striding defiantly up the main street. "Come, child," said her father, "not today: it's late and you're exhausted. You need rest. We'll go first thing tomorrow. I promise."

The entire family climbed the long hill to the cemetery. The brilliant orange sun shone directly into their eyes, so they walked with their heads down, like penitents on their way to a shrine. The mound was located just off the central path toward the back of the graveyard. On the left lay Tato's father and a few other relatives. Three of his brothers had been blown to bits by a Serbian grenade during the first war and what remained of their corpses had become part of the Bosnian soil. His ancestors were buried several kilometers away in the village of Borshiv. And their graves marked the resting places of the illiterate serfs who had, atypically, survived childhood and managed to endure normal working lives. How many more children were rotting in unmarked graves for infants? Scores, perhaps many more. His first wife, Anna, had borne six, none of whom had lived for more than three weeks, until Manya finally hung on to life in Fall River.

He often came here or the Borshiv cemetery on his own, both to pray for the souls of the dead and the souls of the living and to ask God, and himself, whether he had done the right thing to bury Anna and pack their things and take the children home in 1923. Then, it had seemed the only thing to do. Now, with all the devastation that, like Biblical plagues, had befallen this sad land, he decided he should have stayed. Life would have been hard for a widower with three small children, but they would have managed somehow. Their lives might have been confined to the colorful slums of Fall River and he might have had to find work in a soul-crushing mill in order to pay the bills, but there would have been no bombs and guns and prisons and mangled bodies all around them. There would have been life and, even if it were a poor, hungry, and hopeless life, it would still have been better and more hopeful than what they had now. He sighed loudly and Manya and Stefa, who were holding his hands, looked at him attentively. "There it is," he said, pointing at the mound of earth with a wooden cross atop it.

Stefa ran ahead and prostrated herself on the mound. Her stepmother tried to grab her hand—"Don't!" she said. "You'll get your clothes dirty!"—but her father held his wife back and whispered, "Let's pray." Bohdan's mother fell to her knees and placed one trembling hand on the earth. Tato then led the family in an Our Father and a Hail Mary and implored the Lord to embrace

Bohdan and the twenty-one boys who had been sacrificed for their love of country and love of God. "Come, child," he gently coaxed Stefa to her feet. "He's in God's hands now. All we can do is remember him and love him." As Manya embraced Stefa and caressed her cheek, Bohdan's mother dropped her forehead to the gravel path and cried: "Oh, my son, oh, my son! How will I live without you? Why did God take you away from me? How can I possibly exist without you?" "Mama," her daughter said quietly, "Bohdan will live forever. He's a hero and a nation never forgets its heroes." Her mother brusquely pushed her away. "I don't want a hero. I want my Danchyk." Stefa draped her arms around her mother-in-law and led her away. Manya crossed herself three times. Their father looked on and wondered why such a terrible misfortune had befallen his family again.

That evening Stefa took Manya by the hand and suggested they take a walk. The two sisters followed the cow path that led to the stream where the children loved to bathe. On the other side were fields of grain and pasture land that continued for kilometers until they ended at a dense forest. They sat beneath a huge oak tree and watched the last rays of light disappear and the barely illuminated fields turn to shadowy blurs. The crickets and frogs were only just beginning to awaken. "Tell me how he died," Stefa said. "I must know." Manya was silent for several seconds and then, shaking her head, replied, "I think you'd prefer not to know." "Tell me," Stefa insisted. "I have a right to know. I'm his wife—still." "You have a child," Manya said, "you should think about the future, about the child." "Tell me," Stefa repeated. "I have a right to know."

Manya spoke slowly, beginning with the circumstances of Bohdan's arrest in the barber shop and ending with her going to the prison and discovering Bohdan's broken remains at the bottom of the pit. "They shot him first, Stefa. They killed him first because they knew he would never abandon his ideals." "Go on," Stefa said firmly. "And then the men arrayed the corpses on the green grass and—Oh, good Lord, the grass was brown and red from the mud and the blood!—and the people came and identified the bodies and wailing and screaming filled the air and I thought my head would explode. Father Kowcz came and blessed the bodies and performed the last rites"—"Oh, that's good!" Stefa interjected—"and then everyone decided they should be buried properly as quickly as possible, because of the heat and the, well, decomposition."

"The smell must have been terrible," Stefa whispered. "Yes, it was terrible," Manya continued. "The men carried the bodies in clean white sheets and, when the common grave had been dug, they placed the bodies side by side and covered them with earth and built a mound and erected a cross." "Who were the others? How many were there?" "Twenty-one," Manya said. "There was young Prybyla and the three Trofimiaks and Father Bodnar and others we knew and some no one could identify." "And their mothers will never know what happened to their sons!" Stefa cried. "Perhaps that's just as well," Manya said bitterly. "How much death can one endure? How much? Listen, Stefa: I've been thinking a lot about Mykhasko. We pitied him. Remember? The poor, innocent boy cast among the wolves of New York. But just think, Stefa: Mike could've been in that pit as well. Instead, he's alive. Wherever he is, he's alive. When this is all over, you and I and your child—we must all go to Mike." Stefa nodded, saying nothing, and it wasn't clear from the dazed expression on her face that she had even heard her sister's last remarks.

For the rest of the summer and into the fall Stefa ate little, spending most of the day sitting silently at the window or in the garden. When spoken to, she would respond with a slight twist of her lips. Tato, Manya, Slavko, and Fanka made daily efforts to rouse her from her reverie, but she refused to be brought back to a reality that seemed so utterly alien and unnecessary to her. What was the point of life without Bohdan? What was the point of bearing his child? There was none. She should lose the child. It was a sin to think such thoughts, but they streamed unstoppably into her head and seemed perfectly reasonable and desirable. How could a boy grow up without a father? It would be better for him to join his father in Heaven before coming to taste the bitter fruits of life. And what sort of life was this? The boy would be better off if he were spared the misery of loss. In the meantime, she grew and by November it was clear even to her that the child would, alas, be born. Appropriately enough, she went into labor on January 4 and the boy was born on January 5 and Christmas Eve came on January 6 and Christ was born on January 7. It was a sign, of course, and when Stefa looked at the ruddy baby she cradled in her arms, she knew little Bohdan was a miracle granted to her by Providence and that it was her responsibility always to protect the boy from all possible danger.

Stefa spent the next two years tending to the boy. Around her, as arrests, killings, deportations, and executions assumed a quotidian regularity, the world was collapsing once again. Sometime in 1942, Fanka stopped visiting and Manya told her sister that their friend and her parents had gone into hiding and that Vlodko was helping them. That same year, the Germans arrested Father Kowcz and sent him to a death camp in Majdanek. Toward the end of 1943 gunshots increasingly resounded in the middle of the night and Stefa would often awaken, terrified, and hug little Bohdan more closely to her breast. Then, in the first half of 1944, her Polish relatives stopped leaving their homes after sunset. Polish and Ukrainian squads were trading gunfire and it became unsafe to walk the streets. At times, the acrid smell of burning settlements and livestock wafted in the direction of Pocztowa and Tato and Manya shook their heads silently when Stefa asked what was going on.

There was talk of the Russians who were pushing back the Germans and advancing relentlessly across Ukraine. As summer arrived and the burning sun parched people's lips and blurred their vision, rumor had it that the Red Army was only a week or two away. Manya and Slavko told Stefa they intended to flee west and that she, as the wife of an enemy of the people, should join them. "We'll go to Mykhasko," Manya said, "and we'll finally be reunited." "And Tato?" Stefa asked. "Tato will stay here," Manya said sadly. "He says he's too old and will live out his days here, at home. We

137

have to go, Stefa. There's too much death here. Life in America can only be better. Our little brother will help us. And Bohdan will grow up without fear of the NKVD." It was a few weeks later, in mid-July, as the Soviet cannon could be heard somewhere to the east, that the three siblings and the boy said good-bye to their family and their town and, carrying two small suitcases and a few food parcels, boarded a rickety truck headed west.

The day before their departure Manya and Stefa asked their father to accompany them to Borshiv, to the graveyard. "Let's go on foot," Manya suggested. "I want to see this land one last time." They set out in the early morning, walked down Pocztowa, and came to the stream, which they crossed by removing their shoes and wading through the knee-high water; just beyond it was the road that veered to the right to the village. "Let's go through the fields, Tato," Stefa suggested. The sun had not yet reached its apex in the sky, but negotiating the uneven furrows, brushing aside the lusciously golden wheat, and avoiding the cow dung in the pasture land produced streams of sweat and exhausted them. In a clearing at the top of a small rise they sat down on the thick grass and ate crab apples and hardboiled eggs and drank chamomile tea from a thermos.

They reached the village just before noon. The peasants were resting in the fields and children were playing and in the distance they could hear volleys of cannon-fire. The graveyard was smaller than Przemyślany's, but it, too, was neatly maintained. Most of the graves were marked with simple iron crosses: they were rusted and tilted and the names and dates that had been painted on the oval metal plaques had fallen victim to the rains and snows of the last hundred years. Their father still remembered where most of the family lay buried. The barely legible male names were written in Latin: Petrus, Gregorius, Andreas, Paulus, Simeon, Josephus, Nicolaus, Constantinus, Stephanus, Basilius, Joannes, Eustachius, Theodorus, and Demetrius. The women had names that appeared to be Greek: Agafya, Theodora, Eudoxia, Theodosia, Pelagia,

Parasceva, Xenia, Tatianna, Catharina, Anastasia, and the ubiquitous Maria.

"Who are these people?" Manya asked Tato. "How are they related to us?" He said nothing for a few seconds and then confessed: "I don't know. They are your great and great-great and great-great-great grandparents, but just which relative is who I don't know." Again he paused. "It doesn't matter, after all. This is where our family began and it is thanks to them that we are alive today. Never forget that, my daughters." He rubbed his eyes with his sleeve. "Your mother should be buried in this land as well. Visit her in Fall River. She is lonely without us." And then Manya said: "She shouldn't have died, Tato. She should have stayed with us and then we would have stayed with her." "It's God's will," the old man replied. "It's God's will and it's not for us to question His judgment. And now let's go. Tomorrow you embark on a long journey. May God be with you, my sweet daughters, my darling daughters. May God be with you."

As Przemyślany disappeared behind the bend, Stefa couldn't have known that, within a few years, most of the family she was leaving behind would be dead or dispersed. Her grandmother would die in 1945, her father would die in 1949, one Ukrainian branch of the family would be deported to Kazakhstan in 1948 and would return to a country they no longer recognized in 1958, and the Polish side of the family would flee Ukrainian guerrillas later in the summer of 1944, settle in the newly-acquired territories of Silesia, and never return. Fanka would survive, become a Greek Catholic nun, and eventually settle down in Przemyślany as a piano teacher in the local music school. Her paramour Vlodko would commit suicide after his bunker would be surrounded by Soviet secret police units in Prybyn, a tiny village south of Przemyślany. He would be buried there and Fanka would visit him every year and place flowers on his unmarked grave. Many years later, a monument would be erected to Father Kowcz in the cemetery. By the late forties, Przemyślany would have lost almost all the people who inhabited it before the war and become populated by peasants, refugees, and settlers from other parts of Ukraine, Poland, and the Soviet Union: frightened farmers and Soviet acolytes with no memories and no experiences rooted in the town's past. As Przemyślany disappeared behind the bend, Stefa was actually watching it vanish, never to return. It was just as well that she was leaving. The only thing about the town that wouldn't change was the graveyard. It grew inexorably.

The journey began as an adventure and a blessing: anything seemed preferable to waiting for the Red Army and the hated secret police to begin killing again. Very soon, however, it turned into an ordeal. Streams of panic-stricken refugees carrying bundles, suitcases, and children clogged the roads, especially west of Lviv. The truck crawled along with them and some of the more intrepid and less encumbered refugees jumped onto the front fender, hood, or sideboards. Others begged to be taken on board, but there was no room in the back and the men had to refuse, their voices breaking as they wished desperate women and crying children good luck. The truck broke down several times and, as the men tinkered with the motor or patched a tire or the steaming radiator cooled, the interminable waiting would ensue. Fortunately, the abandoned German military vehicles that lined the roads served as convenient sources of spare parts. In the evening, they parked the truck behind some patch of trees, prepared a bonfire, and tried to sleep, some inside, some beneath the stars. Their food supplies ran out after four days, but local peasants were usually happy to provide them with eggs, fat, and bread.

They headed south-west for Sambir and continued in that direction until they could cross the mountains and reach eastern Slovakia. There were rumors that the Carpathians were teeming with Russian, Jewish, and Polish partisans hunting down Ukrainians. A loud truck would attract attention. Besides, they were almost without petrol. After a few minutes' deliberation, they decided to abandon the vehicle and buy a horse and wagon from some peasant. The price was exorbitant: the wily old Ukrainian knew the value of transport in a time of scarcity and sold them a miserable old nag attached to a dilapidated cart that barely seated half of them. He accepted several gold necklaces and wedding rings as payment after laughing at their offers of German money.

The men walked, while the women and children sat in the wagon and endured the ruts and bumps in the pitted earthen road. Half-way up a small mountain, amid the towering pine trees that Manya and Stefa always associated with Mike, they came upon a pile of bloody corpses, mostly men, but also a few women and one child. The flies had settled on their blackened wounds and buzzed with excitement. The blood had dried, but it was obvious that these people had been killed no more than one or two days ago. "No talking," one of the men ordered. "We have to be completely silent. Everyone off the wagon, except for the two women and their infants. And now let's go, in two files."

They walked slowly and silently for several hours. Stefa held Bohdan tightly, while he observed the forest intently and delighted at how the sun cast rays between the treetops and the invisible birds chirped with abandon. When they reached the apex, a plateau-like surface covered with huge slabs of gleaming black rock, they rested for a few minutes in the mid-day sun and then resumed their trek. Squadrons of planes buzzed above them in the azure sky and, as they looked to the east, they caught a last glimpse of the land of their forefathers. "Say good-bye to home," someone said. "Once we start our descent, we'll never see it again." Stefa took Bohdan's little arm and waved it in the direction of Przemyślany. "How do you think Tato is faring?" she asked Manya. "I don't know," her sister said. "We have to think about the future now, about Mike, about leaving this hell for good." As the wagon disappeared into the wood, Bohdan continued waving both hands at the hawks circling above.

Descending the mountain proved more difficult than they expected. The men had to hold the sides of the wagon lest it accelerate and bump the nag. The fits and starts rattled the women inside and, after an hour, they resolved to disembark. Toward three or four in the afternoon, when the sun was already positioned in front of them, a burst of gunfire followed by what appeared to be several grenade explosions greeted them from somewhere to their right. The rat-a-tat of the guns and the booms of the grenades reverberated among the trees and brought the chirping of the birds to a sudden halt. They stopped and, as one of the children began crying, its mother placed her hand across its mouth and implored it to be quiet. Bohdan watched attentively, puzzled by the loud bangs and the silence in the trees. "Should we wait here?" someone asked. "If they find us, they find us and we're dead," someone else said, "so we may as well keep going and reach the bottom sooner rather than later." "Let's go," Manya said. "We are in God's hands. May His will be done." A few hours later they were half-way down the mountain. In the distance golden-domed churches adorned the verdant Slovak countryside. They were safe.

In Prešov, the group disbanded and everyone went his own way. Manya found work as a maid in a little village, Helcmanovce, south-east of Prešov. Stefa and little Bohdan were quartered in Krompachy, a few kilometers north. Little of note happened during their three-year stay in Slovakia. The boy grew and had the usual complement of childhood illnesses. Stefa worked as a seamstress and housecleaner. Manya left for New York first, in early 1947. Stefa and Bohdan joined her and Mike later that year.

Like Manya before them, Stefa and her son boarded a bus at the American embassy in Prague. They traversed all of Germany, crossed by ferry to Sweden, and arrived in Gothenburg, where they boarded the Drottningholm, a gleaming white ship that made Bohdan open his eyes in wonder when he first glimpsed it. They shared a tiny cabin with two other mothers and their children. Stefa spent most of the day sitting on a deck chair, wrapped tightly in two olive-green army blankets and watching the waves rising and falling endlessly. It was the silence and the serenity that held her captive: what a striking contrast to the Slovak household in which she had worked and the country she had last seen three years ago. There were no planes, no cannons, no guns, no graves, and no blood. How unjust, it seemed, to be here, amid so much beauty, while her husband lay beneath a pile of earth in a country that had been repeatedly raped.

She recalled receiving news of his arrest. She recalled the tremor that went through her body as she learned he had been killed. She remembered the endless train ride and the awful sight of the common grave that embraced her poor, dead Bohdan and the despair that engulfed her and led her to want to lose the child. How preposterous that desire now seemed! What else was there in life, what else was there to live for but her son? The boy was sickly and shy, the exact opposite of his father, but she knew that, once they commenced living a normal life under normal conditions, that would change. Once in New York, the boy would come to regard his Uncle Mike, the veteran, as his father. The thought of chubby, little Mykhasko exercising paternal responsibilities amused her and, as she adjusted her sunglasses, she had to laugh.

Little Bohdan roamed the ship and Stefa let him. One of the crew gave the boy his white sailor's cap and Bohdan wore it proudly throughout the day, reluctantly setting it aside only when his mother washed his face and ears. Most of the sailors spoke English and he learned his first words of a language that would soon become his own. "Mama," Bohdan pointed at the waves, "that's o-shen." And, when they were eating in the cafeteria, he said, "That's not *moloko*, Mama, that's meelk." At night, they slept in the same bunk. It was cheaper that way and, besides, Stefa knew the boy would have been too terrified to sleep alone.

Twice, the ship was caught in a fierce storm that drove all the passengers indoors, where they sang folk songs, sewed, played cards or chess, read, or prayed. Bohdan played with the other boys, while Stefa amused herself by reading the names of the passengers and their seat assignments: Ida Eugenia Andersson, Myrtle Ingegerd Berglund, Richard Herman Danielson, Margit Linnea Hegardt, Sigrid Adele Johansson, Maja Ingeborg Norström, Tage Manfred Nyman, Aleksandr and Nadezhda Panfiloff, Martha Svenson,

143

Zdenek Blecha, David Grunberger, Zusana Halas, Reisel, Tauba, and Rachela Halberstam, Juraj Hatala, Emil, Ruzena, and Maximilian Schwarc, Jan and Anna Vajda, Viliam and Heviga Pitzela. Some of the names could have been from Galicia, but most were utterly foreign and the curious arrangement of vowels and consonants was as impossible to pronounce as their language was impossible to understand. She looked out the window at the tall waves and thought: o-shen. And later, when we have supper, I shall have meelk.

This was, she suddenly realized, the second time she was crossing the Atlantic. She had no recollection of the first time, but Manya and Mike loved to tell elaborate stories about their adventures during that trip and it almost seemed as if she had distinct memories of it as well. Was she leaving home or was she going home? It was easier for Mike and Manya to answer that question, because both of them, and especially her sister, could actually visualize America and Fall River in their mind's eye. Manya had been nine when they left; she had even gone to school there and had once spoken English fluently. Mike had been four and claimed to remember a lot as well. America was where they had spent parts of their childhood; it was, Stefa guessed, ultimately their home or, at the very least, their second home. And what of her? She could just as well have been born in Przemyślany. She spoke no English—well, except for o-shen and meelk—and she couldn't remember the mother who always brought tears to Manya's eyes.

Worse, she wasn't even going to Fall River. Her destination was New York, where Mike certainly felt at home by now and Manya had begun working, making a living, and remembering the language of her childhood. She, in contrast, would arrive speechless and penniless. They would be ecstatic to see her, but she had no illusions: it would be difficult for her, probably more difficult than it had been for Mike in 1938. At least the boy would quickly learn the language and adapt to the new world. All children did. He was, it dawned on her, just like Mike. Both had lost a parent and left their homelands at a very young age. Both were withdrawn. Mike eventually became an American soldier—indeed, a sergeant. Would Bohdan follow in his footsteps as well? The poor boy! How would he manage without me in the military? Well, there was enough time to worry about these things later. At the moment, she had other priorities: she would have to send the boy to school—Manya had written there was a Ukrainian school near where they lived—find a job, perhaps as a seamstress, and learn English. O-shen, meelk.

As the ship entered New York harbor, the passengers rushed to the bow to catch a first glimpse of the Statue of Liberty. Boats, ferries, barges, and tugboats zoomed across the dappled surface of the slate water, emerging from all directions out of the creamy mist and seeming to bear down on the Drottningholm before gliding past. They waved to the passengers in the other boats and, sometimes, round sailors in bulky sweaters waved back. "Where is the city?" they cried. "Where is New York? Can anyone see New York and the tall buildings? And where is the statue?" Stefa and Bohdan stood in the bitingly cold air and watched the ship slice the fog. Suddenly, the mournful cawing of invisible gulls ceased, as someone shouted: "*Die Freiheitsstatue! Links! Links!*"—and there, to the left and silhouetted against the gray, stood the green woman on a giant pedestal, her right arm raised high above her head and a torch in her hand—and the crowd produced a deep roar and the roar broke up into cheers and whistles and hurrahs. "We're here, Bohdan," Stefa said breathlessly. "Soon we'll see your Aunt Manya and your Uncle Mykhasko." "Who's that?" the boy asked. "My brother, your uncle," she replied. "You mean Uncle Slavko?" "No," she said, "it's Uncle Mykhasko. He lives here and Aunt Manya lives here and now we'll live with them." "Do they have a garden with apple trees?" "No," she said, "but they live near a park and the park has many trees and slides and swings." "Will they have meelk?" Stefa laughed: "Of course, they'll have meelk, as much as you can drink."

She recognized Manya immediately: she had put on some weight, but who could mistake the dark-haired woman with long eyelashes and brown eyes? Mike, on the other hand, looked completely different from his photographs or how she had imagined him. The baby fat was gone, as were the cautious smile, the innocent eyes, and the hair parted carefully in the middle. Next to Manya stood a handsome young man with wavy hair and a self-confident smile and a cigarette in his hand. As the two sisters embraced, he took Bohdan in his arms and raised him high in the air. "See the gulls?" he asked. "Now you're a gull and we're going to fly home." Manya took the boy and pressed him tightly to her bosom. Stefa stood before Mike and peered into his eyes. "Is this really you?" she gasped. "Am I really here?" Mike produced a hearty laugh and then, to her astonishment, exclaimed in English: "You're damned right you're here, sis! And you're here to stay." "What did you say, Mykhasko? What did you say?" "I think," Manya interjected, "he said we're all together again. Isn't that right, Mike? And we'll always be together. Isn't that right, Mike?" Their brother switched back to Ukrainian: "Sure, that's it exactly. Now stand together right here, just a little to the left. I want to take a photograph of you with the ship in the background."

That evening, as the boy slept, the three siblings sat at the kitchen table drinking tea and eating the apple pastry prepared by Manya. "In a few days," she said, "we'll go to the school and enroll Bohdan in kindergarten. The children all speak Ukrainian, so he should be fine." "He's begun speaking Slovak," Stefa interjected. "Lord, how he's grown since I last saw him! But he'll be fine, Stefa, don't worry. This area is full of our people—some are even from Przemyślany—and he'll easily make friends. And then we have to find you a job. We can ask at the parish office and at church. Cleaning houses is hard work, but I've gotten used to it and so will you. Once we're on our feet, we can find something else, something better. The city is full of textile factories and I'm sure they can use an experienced seamstress. Have another piece. Do you like it?" For a second, Manya paused and looked into her sister's eyes. "Everything is different here, but you'll get used to it quickly. You're young and

Bohdan—well, he'll forget Przemyślany and Krompachy in a few weeks." "He's already forgotten Przemyślany," Stefa said drily.

"I can hardly remember it myself," Mike added. "This is a great country, Stefa. I love it! I really do. And you'll love it, too. They treat you well here. And everything is possible. I mean, look at me. I've been out west, I've handled jackhammers, exploded mountains, built roads, learned to march, learned to shoot. I'm a soldier, Stefa. Can you believe your little Mykhasko is a soldier, a veteran, that I actually served in the army and have medals to prove it?" He tapped his chest. "It's a great country, Stefa. You can be a human being here. You can be free here. Isn't that right, Manya?" His sister looked at him quietly. "Don't worry, Manya, I'll find a job soon. I'm a veteran and I've got skills. I just have to keep looking and I'll find something." Mike rose from the table and extended his arms. "It's a great country, Stefa. Isn't that right, Manya? Have you heard this song?

They said someday you'll find
All who love are blind
Oh, when your heart's on fire
You must realize
Smoke gets in your eyes

"It's about me, Stefa. It's about finding what you've been looking for. Don't worry, Manya. I'll find it."

As they lay in bed, Stefa asked her sister if Mike was well. "He's changed so much," she said. "I can barely recognize him. And he goes on and on about America and his jobs. Is he always this nervous, this incoherent?" "I think," Manya replied, "that Mike experienced something terrible in the army. He doesn't want to talk about it. He refuses to talk about the last four years. I've asked him many times to tell me what it was like, but he just smiles and turns away. Something happened. I don't know what, but something happened and it couldn't have been good." Manya paused. "He has

147

nightmares, Stefa. And several times I've heard him scream a woman's name: Wanda." She paused again. "There must have been a girl." "Yes," Stefa said, "you're right. Our brother must have fallen in love with a Polish girl who left him for some other soldier." "He tries to act more self-confidently," Manya added, "but he's really the same Mykhasko we've always known. He's just a sensitive, frightened, little boy, you know. He'll be fine, I know he will, especially now that we're all together again. And did you notice his camera? It's become an obsession with him." "Yes," replied Stefa, "he seemed very professional about the way he photographed us today." "But did you know," Manya added, "that there was no film in the camera?"

The boy went to school and learned how to play stickball, Stefa got a job cleaning houses in the Bronx, Manya found employment as a secretary in a Ukrainian insurance company in Jersey City, and Mike remained without work. He and little Bohdan became best friends and Mike took him around the neighborhood, showed him the exact layout of the terrifyingly large park next door, and, after Bohdan came home one day with a bloody nose, took him aside and taught him how to fight. "I used to be just like you," he said, "but the only way to stand up to a tough guy is to fight back." And he showed Bohdan how to throw a punch and how to dodge one and what to do if he was knocked to the ground and when to recognize defeat and run. "But, even then," he said, "even when you know you've lost, never cry, never give the other guy the satisfaction of having made you cry. Understood?"

Increasingly, as the boy's school days became longer and he found new friends, Mike took to sitting in his room or pressing his ear to the radio or walking the streets with his camera and taking phantom photographs. The rest of the story has been told. His nightmares worsened, his singing increased, and his obsession with his camera and Wanda-Edna grew. When he cut his veins and almost jumped from the roof, the sisters knew they had to act and, in 1951, at the age of thirty-one and some eight months, Mike was taken to Bellevue. Meanwhile, Manya got married and had two children, Stefa got married and moved to an apartment on Eighth Street, while Bohdan finished high school, found a job, and, as Stefa had once surmised, was drafted into the U.S. Army. The sisters visited their mother's grave in Fall River in 1952 and then every ten years thereafter. Bohdan, Manya, and Stefa passed away in 2011-2012, more than fifteen years after Mike died, of old age and a broken life and without his camera, in a veterans' hospital on Long Island. The doctors knew him as the genial patient who wandered along the corridors and gardens and continually sang a song that only some of them had heard of:

> *They said someday you'll find*
> *All who love are blind*
> *Oh, when your heart's on fire*
> *You must realize*
> *Smoke gets in your eyes*

The absence of memories and experiences is notable, of course, but the beginnings, middles, and ends are in place and form something in the nature of a coherent narrative. All that remains is to ask one final, unanswerable question: Did thirty-two-year old Jan-Ivan have any idea, as he boarded the ship to New York in 1913, that it would all end and begin and end in Fall River?

Alexander J. Motyl (b. 1953, New York) is a writer, painter, and professor. Nominated for the Pushcart Prize in 2008 and 2013, he is the author of six published novels, *Whiskey Priest*, *Who Killed Andrei Warhol*, *Flippancy*, *The Jew Who Was Ukrainian*, *My Orchidia*, and *Sweet Snow*. *Ardor House*, his eighth, is forthcoming in 2015. His poems have appeared in 34th Parallel, The Battered Suitcase, Counterexample Poetics, Istanbul Literary Review, The Green Door, The Literary Bohemian, Mayday, New York Quarterly, Orion Headless, Red River Review, and Red Savina Review. He is currently working on a satire of intellectuals, policy makers, and businesspeople called *Ardor House*. He has done performances of his fiction and poetry at the Cornelia Street Café, the Bowery Poetry Club, the Ukrainian Institute of Modern Art in Chicago, the Ukrainian Museum in New York, and a variety of universities. For several years, Motyl collaborated with Ultra Violet, the recently deceased Andy Warhol Superstar, on a play, "Andy vs. Adolf." He is also author of a one-line play, *Waiting by Godot*. Motyl's artwork is part of the permanent collections of The Ukrainian Museum in New York City and the Oseredok Ukrainian Educational and Cultural Centre in Winnipeg; his works have been displayed in solo and group shows in New York City, Philadelphia, and Toronto and are on display on the Internet gallery, www.artsicle.com. He teaches in the political science department at Rutgers University-Newark and is the author of six academic books, numerous scholarly and policy articles, and a weekly blog on "Ukraine's Orange Blues" on www.worldaffairsjournal.org. Motyl lives in New York City

34492267R00086

Made in the USA
Charleston, SC
10 October 2014